I0550341

The
Unleashed
Series
Book 1

THE

ARTIFICIAL

WITCH

LEE K. ROGERS

Open Door Publications

The Artificial Witch
The Unleashed Series Book 2

Copyright © 2025 by Lee K. Rogers

ISBN: 979-8-9871697-4-2

This is a work of fiction. Names, characters, places, and incidents are either a product of the author's imagination or are used fictitiously. Any resemblance to actual events, or persons or locales, living or dead, is purely coincidental.

Published by
Open Door Publications
Willow Spring, NC 27592
www.OpenDoorPublications.com

Cover Design: Eric Labacz, www.labaczdesign.com

For Sherri, Janice, and Wendy who have faithfully read and critiqued my books—even when they knew nothing about werewolves, witches or vampire. Thanks for following me into the foreign land of the paranormal and giving me great feedback.

Prologue

Moonlight flickered in the clearing as the clouds crisscrossed its surface, turning everything black, then highlighting the new leaves on the trees and changing the spring flowers that were sprinkled in the grass to silver. It picked out the makeshift altar hastily set up and then abandoned in the middle of the grassy knoll.

A wandering deer moved closer to the platform, intrigued by the scent of the girl who lay on the stones. Her blonde hair was carefully brushed; her makeup was flawless. The markings painted on her body glistened, turning from deep crimson to black as they dried. She looked peacefully asleep until one moved closer and saw the knife wound carved in the shape of a pentagram on her torso.

CHAPTER 1

Three bodies in three months. Shannon Kelly shook her head with disgust. Here she was again, standing guard duty outside another murder scene. This wasn't what she'd come to Rivelou for, and today, on top of everything else, it was hot. Way too hot for the first day of May in western Kentucky. The temperature was going to reach 90 degrees today, and at nine o'clock in the morning the sun was already beating down on the picnic clearing in Rivelou's Northside City Park, which was known for its ancient Native American burial mounds.

"Move along, please," Shannon said to the two joggers who had been drawn to the flashing red lights of three police cruisers, an ambulance, and just arriving, an SUV with the emblem of the county coroner on the side. She took off her Rivelou PD cap and wiped her forehead, wondering why she had wanted to move almost three hundred miles south of Chicago. There, according to the weather app on her phone, the temperature today was a delightful 60 degrees with no humidity. To make matters worse, Shannon was wearing a Kevlar vest, a gear belt with pepper spray, Taser, baton, radio and cell phone, plus two firearms. And of course, to make the fashion statement complete, steel toed boots.

The joggers she had motioned to reluctantly moved a few feet from the yellow tape line and joined the growing crowd of spectators. How did so many people have nothing to do on a weekday morning? Why weren't they at work? Or school? Or posting cat videos on Facebook? Anything but standing around here asking stupid questions she wouldn't be able to answer, she thought with a sigh as she noticed a television truck topped with a satellite dish slowly pulling into the parking area next to the picnic pavilion.

Just then the coroner, Dr. Nathan Lazard, hopped out of his vehicle and waved hello to her. She glanced at him appreciatively; he was in his late thirties, several inches over six feet tall, and made a habit of wearing all black. Did he think that was the appropriate dress for a coroner, or was it just that he knew he looked good in black? It made a great contrast with his blonde hair and fair skin she thought as she idly checked him out. His wardrobe today was a black, long-sleeved dress shirt and black silk tie with black, boot-cut jeans. Of course, black sunglasses completed the look, obscuring his eyes. Why wasn't he sweating in this heat? It was definitely unfair, Shannon decided.

"What have we got? Shannon Kelly isn't it?" he asked as he approached, his Cajun accent prominent.

"Yeah, it's Shannon, Dr. Lazard. And I don't know what we've got. They haven't let me past the yellow tape. I'm just on guard duty."

He obviously heard the disgust in her voice. "Don't let it get to you, *cher*. Sometimes it's better to be on this side of the yellow tape. And call me Nathan." He smiled, gave her a quick pat on the shoulder, and hurried past.

Now what, she wondered, had that been all about? He'd never really spoken to her before. She turned and took a second look at the doctor. "Nice eye candy," she thought again as she appreciatively watched him walk away.

She hadn't realized the coroner knew who she was. Shannon had seen him on her last two crime scenes. Two murders, one in February and one in March, and of course that thing in October. She'd actually been at more than just a couple of murder scenes in the past few months, a lot more than expected. She had moved here because Rivelou was supposed to be a quieter, less... well violent... place to be a police officer than Chicago.

So far, that hadn't proven to be the case. She'd already been involved in more bizarre deaths than she'd ever experienced in five years on the Chicago Police force.

Shannon shook her head and got back to reality. She lifted her cap again, shook out her short, blonde curls, and wiped the sweat from her brow.

She could just hear her partner, Office David Thorne, talking with the coroner and the detective in charge, Tony Abello, but couldn't make out any of the words. It pissed her off that

Dave was over there looking over the crime scene while she was on crowd control. And there were just enough bushes in the way that she couldn't even get a glimpse of what was going on.

Yeah, Abello had been Dave's partner before he was promoted to detective at the first of the year, and she was still considered a newcomer to the department even though she'd worked there a little over a year now. But she'd learned that, although Rivelou was large enough to bear the title of "city," in many ways it was just as clannish as any small, Southern town. Which meant that sometimes the fact that she had five years' worth of experience with the Chicago police force before moving here meant a lot less in Rivelou than Dave's two years as the partner of the detective in charge of the current investigation.

She sighed again. If there was one thing she had already learned about living and working in Rivelou, it was that it wasn't always about what you knew, but about who you knew.

Well, that had been to her advantage last October during the incident with Professor Alexander Fontaine. The well-known author and professor was still on the official missing persons list, even though she, the chief of police, and a few other people in town, including her brother Chris and his fiancée, Ana, knew the man wasn't missing. He was dead.

No. She shook her head to dispel the memory; she didn't want to think about it again. That murder site had been grisly. She would just focus on today's crime scene. She wasn't going to get distracted thinking about anything else right now. Instead, she put her energy into attempting to hear what was being said as her fellow police officers and the coroner looked at the dead body that had been found early this morning by a couple walking their dog.

"Not like any markings I've ever seen. And similar, but not exactly like the last ones either." She heard a few words in her partner's voice. "But I can check…"

"Officer Kelly, isn't it?"

She lost the rest of the low-voiced conversation behind her when the news reporter stepped up. "Officer Kelly. Alicia Myers, remember me? Can you tell me what's going on?"

"Sorry, ma'am. You know I can't say anything. The

media liaison hasn't arrived yet. You'll have to wait until he gets here to get an official statement."

It hurt Shannon just a little to call the young twit of a reporter ma'am. She had to be barely out of college. But Shannon had learned that the media should always be treated formally, even a little distantly. If you got too friendly with them, they just took advantage.

"Shannon, c'mon. You know me. I won't use anything you tell me on the record. Just give me a little something to go on. Is this like the last two murders? Young, college-age women? Do we have a serial killer on our hands?"

Right, she thought sarcastically. She was going to answer the reporter's questions and get quoted as an unnamed source on the evening news. It wouldn't take anyone long to figure out who had talked even if the reporter didn't use her name. They were cops, after all. Investigating was what they did. As soon as it was clear that she was the one who had talked, it would be a quick trip to the unemployment office. Alicia Myers already seemed to know more than the police department had put out in their press statements. Officially, the last two deaths were still just that: deaths. Only police officers were supposed to know that the coroner had declared them murders. Myers obviously had some good sources.

Even before these recent incidents the reporter had been following the trail of the Professor Fontaine disappearance with great fervor. She had somehow learned that Shannon had been at his apartment building the last night he had been seen, and she'd approached Shannon several times to try to get her to talk about what had happened that night.

Well, that was never going to happen. Talk about a good way to lose your job.

"Sorry, ma'am. You can see just as much from here as I can," Shannon said to the reporter, waving her hand toward the bushes and picnic shelter that obscured most of the scene. Again, she knew the resentment showed in her voice and hoped Alicia didn't notice. Dave was over there as a part of the investigation while she was babysitting reporters and joggers. No matter what Dr. Nathan Lazard had said, it still stung.

She had nothing against Dave. They'd been partners for almost six months now, and she couldn't complain. He was a good partner. But, in Shannon's eyes, he was still wet behind the ears. He'd turned thirty a few weeks ago. And celebrated with a party that showed just how young he was. She'd joined him and his friends on the party bus he had hired for a short time but had soon grown bored.

She was thirty-three, not that much older. But she had felt as if she were ancient compared to Dave and all of his friends. She was a widow, for god's sake. Didn't just saying that word make her older, somehow? It certainly made her feel that way.

Behind her she heard the group breaking up.

"How the hell did she get here?" she heard Tom Jackson, one of the cops who had been allowed closer to the murder scene, say. "Just like the others. There's no car, no bike, no tracks even, to show a car has been here in days. It's a dirt road back here, and it rained yesterday. There should be something."

"Transported by fairies?" his partner, Steven Sanservino answered jokingly. "You never know in this town."

"And you know enough not to say stuff like that," Jackson retorted.

Shannon heard them and raised her eyebrows. It was rare to hear anyone in Rivelou admit that there was anything different about the community.

The Chamber of Commerce called Rivelou "The River City" and promoted it as a hub of the Kentucky/Indiana/Illinois triangle, convenient to everything. Convenient to almost nothing was more like it, Shannon snorted. Half a day's drive from everywhere. But, she admitted to herself, that was why she had come here. She had wanted a place that was quiet and out of the way. After her husband, Jason, had died in Chicago two years ago she had thought that Rivelou was the perfect place to heal. It was supposed to be a quiet town where nothing much happened, where being a cop meant handing out parking tickets and making sure the college frat parties didn't get too loud and disorderly.

Boy, had she been wrong. Here she was at her fifth murder scene in less than a year. And she was learning that this was pretty much the way things rolled in Rivelou.

The first murder scene she had been at, the one back in September, hadn't been classified as a murder. It was called a dog attack. The dog was never found. Only she and a handful of other people knew who the real killer had been. And what had happened to him. Which was why she had been at the scene of the second murder—well justifiable homicide really. She'd have been dead herself along with her brother, Chris, if her soon-to-be sister-in-law hadn't arrived in time to save the day by turning into a werewolf and killing Fontaine, the rogue shapeshifter who had been responsible for the first murder as well as that of her husband back in Chicago.

But officially Professor Alexander Fontaine wasn't even dead. Yeah, life in Rivelou was nothing like she had imaged it would be.

CHAPTER 2

Shannon's thoughts were interrupted by her partner, Dave. He looked a little green around the gills. Obviously, he hadn't been prepared to see a dead body this morning.

Dave was a nice guy and a pleasure to look at. Tall and dark, with a close-cropped dark beard. He stood a little over six feet: lean, with muscles that showed he spent a good bit of his free time in the gym. When he wasn't racing around town on his Harley, that was.

"Got some water?" he asked.

"Yeah, right here," she said, taking a small water bottle out of one of her pockets. "You're looking a little pale."

"It was bad. I haven't seen too many bodies cut up like that."

Shannon nodded toward where Alicia Myers had been joined by a few of other reporters, two men and a woman. They were all straining to hear the low-voiced conversation between the two partners. "Be careful what you say. If it ends up on the news today, your ass is grass."

"Yeah, thanks. You're right," Dave said. He took another swig of water, then took off his hat and just poured the rest of the bottle over his head, running his hand through his hair. If Shannon had done that she'd have looked like a drowned rat. How come when Dave did it, his tousled, wet hair just looked sexy?

Shannon saw with irritation that Alicia and a few of the female spectators had noticed, too. She gave herself a mental shake. It didn't matter to her that other women were ogling her partner. Right?

"That feels better," Dave said, putting his cap back on, seemingly oblivious to the stir he had just caused. "C'mon. We can get out of here now."

Once in the car, with Shannon in the driver's seat and the air conditioning going full blast, she asked, "Well, are you going to tell me about it?"

Dave closed his eyes. "You know you are really lucky you didn't have to see it. Like I said, I've never seen a body that torn up. It was worse even than the other two."

"Humph," Shannon snorted. She'd seen a few torn-up bodies—Alexander Fontaine for instance. She could handle it. She had handled it. Dave's reaction just proved that she should have been the officer they pulled in for a consultation, not her partner. She drove out of the parking lot faster than she should have, kicking up gravel and sending the reporters scattering. Good. She couldn't hold back her temper any longer.

"And the girl looked about my cousin's age. Hit me too close to home, I guess. I kept thinking it could have been Winnie."

"Shit, that's rough. I'm sorry about that. Do they have an ID on her yet? Did your cousin know her?"

"Not yet. She was naked. No clothes, no purse. Nothing to tell us who she was."

"So yeah, besides you having a cousin the same age," Shannon couldn't hide the sarcasm in her voice, "what's so special about you that you got to consult with the coroner and the detective? Just because you're the hometown golden boy doesn't mean..."

"I know you don't think I know anything, Shannon." Dave ran his hand over his beard, as he often did, she'd noticed. This time in obvious frustration. "You make that perfectly clear every chance you get." His voice was a little bitter now, and Shannon suddenly felt guilty. She hadn't realized her feelings toward the man had been so obvious. "I do have some areas of expertise that you do not."

"Oh yeah?" She tried to soften her tone—wasn't sure if it was working. She took a breath and tried again. "So, what's your expertise?" *Asking was playing nice, wasn't it?*

"The body had some marks on it; the last two bodies did too. They wanted to know if I'd seen anything like them."

Now she was intrigued. "What kind of marks?"

"Tattoos."

"You're a tattoo expert?" She was surprised. And

intrigued. Dave, who looked and acted like the clean-cut boy next door despite the motorcycle, was a tattoo expert?

"I've got a couple," he admitted.

"Hmm." Shannon was now definitely intrigued. It was a small department. There was only one locker room. That meant she had seen a good bit of Dave's very good-looking flesh, but she'd never noticed anything other than one Celtic band tattoo on his upper arm.

He grinned. He had finally gotten the attention of Officer I Know Everything Because I'm from Chicago Kelly. "Want to see?" he asked, his hand sliding suggestively to his belt buckle.

She put her hand up. "No way! TMI!" She chuckled appreciatively. Dave had managed to dispel her bad mood. "But seriously," she added as she continued the drive back downtown to City Hall and police headquarters, "Tell me the rest of it. What was it about this body? I know I sometimes act like I think you're a rookie, but I do know you've seen stuff before. Why did this one affect you so much? You really looked like you were about to puke back there."

"It was bad, Shannon. She was cut from stem to stern. The doc says probably while she was still alive. It looked like some kind of ritual killing. And her heart was gone. Taken right out of her chest."

"Wow! I see what you mean. That's really…" Shannon made a face as she tried to come up with the right word, then gave up. Just hearing the description was bad. "No wonder it bothered you."

"Yeah, the doc said it looked to him like it was some kind of ceremony. But it wasn't anything like I'd seen before."

"What do you mean? Why would you have seen something like that before?"

"It was staged to look like a Beltane ceremony. But it wasn't. And the other murders—they were similar but not exactly like this one. It wasn't real. As if someone had read all the books but didn't really have any experience, didn't actually know what they were doing. If it had been done by true practitioners, each of the ceremonies would have adhered to strict rituals, not to mention that nobody would have been sliced open and killed."

"What makes you say that? How would you know what a real Beltane ceremony looks like?"

"Shannon. C'mon. You've been my partner for months now. You must have heard some of the other cops talking about me."

"No. Remember. I'm the new cop from Chicago. Your Rivelou pals don't gossip about you to me. So, what are we talking about here?"

"I'm a witch."

CHAPTER 3

"You're a what? C'mon Dave, don't joke with me." Shannon chuckled again. She tried to hide the sick feeling she suddenly had in the pit of her stomach. She was determined not to let it show. "I thought you rode a Harley to work, not a broomstick."

"Shannon. I'm perfectly serious. I'm a witch. I thought, you, of all people, would have figured it out."

Shannon pulled into traffic as she shot Dave a questioning look. She really didn't like where this conversation was heading. "What do you mean, 'me, of all people?'" she said with an edge to her voice.

Dave was familiar with that tone and look. It meant Shannon didn't want to talk about something. And most of the time he backed off. It hadn't taken too many weeks as Shannon's partner to learn that she was a very, very private person. She kept distance between herself and the other men and women on the force. She was friendly enough outwardly, but if anyone ever tried to get the least bit close to her, she quickly shut them off and shut them out.

He didn't think she even realized that other people thought of her as prickly and hard to get to know. She didn't seem to notice how often she put up barriers, making it clear to the other cops on the force that she had things she didn't want to discuss. Like her dead husband who'd been a cop in Chicago, or that mess last fall with the professor from the University of Rivelou, or that her brother was now engaged to a shapeshifter… Yeah, there were a lot of things Shannon Kelly didn't like to discuss.

But Dave wasn't going to let her get away with it this time. There were things about this case that made it important for her to no longer keep her distance from everyone else on the Rivelou Police Force. There were others who sensed the same things that he did about Shannon Kelly. Unless she started to acknowledge those things and explain them, and herself, to the powers-that-be, she could find herself a suspect in a chain of very ugly murders.

"You've got power. I can sense it."

"I do not. I mean, I… I don't know what the hell you're talking about," she said, trying to sound huffy, but instead just sounding a little bit scared. It made Dave feel bad; he didn't want to upset her. But he had finally caught her in a slip-up, and he wasn't going to back off this time. She knew exactly what he was talking about. And it was time for her to admit it.

"You've got power. I don't know why you're afraid to use it, or even acknowledge it, but it's obvious that you have it. That's why I've never discussed it with you until now. I could tell it was a subject that you're sensitive about."

"I'm not sensitive about the subject because I don't have any special powers. I'm not a believer." She kept her eyes on the road, not even glancing at him once. She knew she'd slipped up. Every time she tried to protest that she knew nothing about the paranormal, she ended up tacitly admitting that she knew exactly what her partner was talking about.

David sighed. He could feel a few new rows of bricks quickly being added to the wall Shannon had already put up between them. He ran his hand down his face again in frustration. He had worked hard in the last few months since he had become her partner to build a friendship between them. He could sense now that any bit of progress he had made had just been lost.

But he wasn't one to give up so easily. He smiled mischievously, then flicked his left wrist and opened it. A small, bright orange flame burned in his hand.

"What the…" Shannon glanced over, screamed, and slammed on the brakes just as she reached the busy intersection of Main Street and Franklin Avenue. Dave quickly closed his left hand, putting out the flame, while at the same time he made another flicking motion with his right. The pickup truck that had slammed on its brakes behind them came miraculously to a stop a few inches from the bumper of the police cruiser, while the three vehicles already in the intersection sped up instantly and managed to get out of the way. A horn sounded as the driver in the truck behind her drove around the car, rolled down his window, and shouted, "Stupid cops! Don't they teach you how to drive?"

Shannon sat still in the intersection for another few moments, taking deep breaths, staring at Dave with a strange look he could not identify on her face.

"You'd better get going again before someone calls it in," he finally said in a gentle voice. He felt a little guilty. He'd just meant to make her admit what she was, not scare the crap out of her. He grimaced. Sometimes, he knew, his sense of humor got the better of his good sense. Obviously, this had been one of those times, and now, instead of loosening up, Shannon might very well quit talking to him altogether.

For now, though, she obeyed his request to get a move on. Her hands were only a little bit shaky on the wheel as she stepped on the gas and headed downtown toward headquarters.

"Why would you do something like that?" she complained, her hands now gripping the wheel so tightly that her knuckles were white. "That was idiotic. You scared the hell out of me, David!"

Yeah, he felt a little guilty, but he wasn't going to back off from the conversation now that they had finally started it. Shannon needed to come out of the closet right now or things were going to get really hot for her. He'd seen the glances a couple of the cops at the scene, including his ex-partner, Tony, had given her.

"You said you didn't believe in magic. I just wanted to show you a little. I figured you'd seen the fire thing before. After all, it is the first thing a young witch learns."

Shannon took a deep breath. "Okay, you're right. I've seen it before. My mother used to make me practice it every day when I was kid." The words poured out. Now that she had admitted that, not only did she believe in magic, she had powers herself, she wanted to get it all out in the open and be done with it.

"She always told me how talented I was. That I could do anything with it, make people do anything I wanted them to, give me anything I wanted. That's how she used it. She used it for power over other people. I'm not going to do that. I've given up all that stuff. I saw what she did with magic, and it was nothing good, believe me. If you practice magic like she did, I don't want anything to do with it."

Or you. Shannon didn't need to say that out loud. Her message was perfectly clear. David decided to ignore it.

"So, your mom was the witch in the family. What about your dad?"

"He left shortly after I was born when he found out what my mother was. We never saw him again. At least that's what Mom always said. When I got older, I started to wonder if my mom had more to do with his disappearance than she told us. She wasn't the kind of person to just let someone who had hurt her walk away without making them pay."

"Well, that explains a lot," Dave said.

"What do you mean by that?" she asked with a challenge in her voice.

"It's obvious to anyone with power that you're a witch, but you don't practice. You don't talk about it. You haven't approached anyone on the force with power to ask about joining with us. There're times we could use the help of another magic practitioner. We've given you your space, but we did wonder. And now it's getting serious. If you don't explain…"

"If I don't explain what?" Shannon cut him off. "And how can you tell I have power anyway? No wait," she brushed her initial questions aside with a wave of her hand as another thought struck her. "What you mean is that you were gossiping about me!" Her voice rose in indignation. "What gives you, or anyone else in the Rivelou P.D., the right to talk about me behind my back?"

"Whoa! Wait a minute. No one's gossiping about you." He sighed in frustration and acknowledged, "Well, okay, we have gossiped, but no more than we gossip about anyone else," he amended with a small smile. "And we work in situations where we've got to depend on each other. And you've made it very clear that you don't want to talk about yourself. Shit! I don't mean… it's just…" Dave stuttered to a stop, figuring there wasn't too much more he could say to make things worse than they already were.

But Shannon ignored his gaffe. "You said 'if I don't explain.' What do I have to explain, and why is it anyone else's business? My private life is just that—private. I shouldn't have to explain anything to anyone."

"Not usually. That's why we've all kept quiet and left you alone. Until now. But with these murders…"

"What do these murders have to do with me and whether or not I have power?"

"Well, they're obviously being done by someone who knows a little bit about witchcraft, but not enough. Someone untrained." Dave winced and rubbed his hand across his face. The conversation had just gone from bad to worse.

"You mean I'm a suspect," Shannon said in a quiet, even tone that Dave found even worse than her earlier indignation. He closed his eyes for a moment, thinking about how not to offend his prickly partner any more than he already had. Finally, he opened his eyes, let out a breath, and started to answer, but at that minute the radio crackled. "Car 15, a burglary reported at 2501 Maple Avenue."

Shannon turned on the siren and hit the gas pedal. "Don't think this conversation is over," she said ominously.

CHAPTER 4

They dealt with the reported burglary, Shannon frostily polite to Dave the entire time. It turned out to be nothing more than some misplaced garden equipment. Mrs. Andres, the elderly woman who had made the report, had forgotten that she had put her wheelbarrow, hoe, and other tools in her garage so she could easily work with them again rather than locking them in her garden shed as she usually did.

Shannon had dealt with the woman before. She was a neighbor of her soon-to-be sister-in-law, Ana. She was known as a gossip and a busybody, if a harmless one. Shannon suspected she sometimes called the police just because she was lonely. By the time they got back to the car, Shannon seemed to have relented just a little toward her partner. "Now this is the kind of crime I thought I was going to have to deal with when I moved to Rivelou. Nice, easy, non-violent stuff. Not murder," Shannon said as she and Dave continued to patrol the quiet, tree-lined streets with their neat brick or white frame houses. "Or witchcraft. I think you'd better start to explain more about what you meant earlier."

Yeah, I knew I wasn't getting off that easily. "Okay. You deserve to know. In fact, you really need to know." Dave took a breath and tried to figure out where to start. "It's obvious to anyone on the force with power that..."

"Wait a minute! You said, 'anyone on the force with power.'" She cut across his explanation again. "You mean there are other witches in the department?" She glanced curiously at him but quickly turned her eyes back to the road. One almost traffic accident was enough for one day.

"Not just witches. A couple of shapeshifters, a siren, and Dr. Lazard of course. He's a vampire."

Shannon's mouth fell open at that.

"Come on, Shannon, don't be naïve. You have to have felt the power around the office."

"No. I haven't. I cut that part of my life off. I've blocked it out. Literally blocked my ability to use magic. I don't even pay attention to it anymore." She was over-explaining, and she knew it. Dave could see it in her expression. He shook his head.

"It's a part of you. How can you just cut it off? It would be like cutting off my right hand if I ignored my power."

"It's something that's never brought anything good to my life. Why would I want it? Power made my mother evil. Power—well, okay, not witchcraft but another paranormal creature with a different kind of power—took my husband away from me. Why would I want anything to do with your kind of power?"

"Your husband? I didn't know that. I thought he was killed on the job?"

"No. Well, yes, he was on the job. But he was killed by a werewolf. Alexander Fontaine."

"Oh. Wow. I didn't know. So that's why... maybe you'd better explain some things to me first," Dave said slowly.

"When it happened, I was told very pointedly not to talk about it, but, yeah, well... I guess it's time we get some things out in the open."

She took a deep breath and began. "My husband—Jason—always wanted to be a cop. Ever since he was a teenager. We'd known each other since high school; he was my brother's best friend. Chris doesn't have much power; you see, he was never very good at spells or controlling the power he did have, so our mom pretty much ignored him growing up."

Dave made a small sound of distress. "I guess that sucked for him."

. "Oh, she didn't abuse him or anything. She never used her magic on him. She had that much maternal feeling, I guess. And as we got a little older, we both agreed he was the lucky one. I was the one who had to be perfect. She just ignored Chris. It didn't matter to her that he got all As in school or that he was on the baseball team. So, he kind of spent all his time at Jason's house. And I spent as much time there as I could, too.

"I was the talented one, so I got all my mother's attention. And I didn't want it. Oh yeah, when I was little it was cool, learning how to make fire, how to control the elements. The wind… I really loved that. It gave me such a sense of being in control, you know?"

She looked over at Dave with a wistful smile that tugged at his heart. He could see the girl she had been, a young girl who had little love and less security in her life, learning that she could control the forces of nature.

"But as I got older," Shannon continued, cutting into Dave's thoughts, "I saw just how my mother used her magic. And I didn't want it. I didn't want to learn what she did. She used spells to trick other people into giving us money, or to make herself irresistible to someone else's husband, or to bring someone she believed had harmed her bad luck. And anytime something didn't go her way she always said it was someone else's fault and the things that she'd do for revenge…"

Shannon stopped and took a breath. It was obvious to Dave that she hadn't talked about this in years; it was as if once she started, she couldn't stop. They passed a church parking lot, empty on a weekday afternoon. "Maybe you should pull over here and tell me the rest of this," he said, motioning toward the lot. "Only one near-accident allowed per day, remember?"

"Yeah. Okay," she said with a tiny laugh as she pulled into the empty lot and radioed in that they were taking a break. Then she turned toward Dave and continued.

"So, to make a long story short, I saw that power corrupts, so I vowed never to use my powers. I guess, in a way, that's part of why I became a cop. I saw how my mother had wronged people, and I wanted to help people who had been wronged.

"Anyway, when Chris and I graduated from high school we left home. W…we haven't seen our mother since that day."

"She let you go that easily?"

"Yeah, well no. It wasn't that easy." Shannon turned her head. She couldn't look David in the eyes. There were things about that last night at her mom's house he didn't need to know. She'd only told Jason, not even Chris.

She took a breath and continued. "Jason and I went to the police academy, and then we got married. Chris, well I guess you know about him, too. He knew too much about the dark side of power to let it go, and he has enough power to track the dark things: vampires, shapeshifters, witches—any creature who is doing evil. In fact, it seems to be where his talent lies. When he's hunting is when he's most in control of his magic."

"Yeah, I know he's a Hunter. I guess everyone in the department knows that. Some of them are kind of suspicious of him, but he seems like a good guy. It's still kind of a mystery how he ended up with Hank Bertrand's granddaughter as his fiancée. I mean, a Hunter and the granddaughter of the Alpha of a shapeshifter clan. It's kind of a stretch, ya' know?"

"Yeah, well think about it from my side." Shannon shook her head. "I wasn't too thrilled about his choice of fiancée at first, either. With our upbringing and Chris's job, we haven't seen much good in people with power or paranormal abilities. We wanted to stop the monsters."

"But what does all this have to do with your husband?" Dave asked to bring her back to her story. Now that he'd gotten her to talk about herself, he certainly didn't want to get her off track.

"That's what happened to Jason; he was trying to stop a monster." She took a deep breath. It had been almost two years, but it was still hard for her to talk about. "Jason and I were both with the Chicago Police. He worked downtown, near the Loop. My precinct was on the South Side.

"Jason and I started noticing there were several reports each month of a large dog, or possibly a wolf, being seen around Grant Park. The animal would appear for a few days, then not be seen for a couple of weeks. No one was bitten. At first. He just scared people. And no one seemed to be able to catch the dog.

"Jason and I started keeping track of the incidents. We knew the significance of the timing; the dog was always seen at the full moon and never at any other time.

"Then, one of the women he attacked was bitten. She went through the whole series of rabies shots." Shannon shook her head as if at such foolishness. "Jason and I knew that was useless, but who were we going to tell? What could we say? No one was going to believe us, anyway. I tried to keep my eye on the woman. I wanted to see if whoever had bitten her would approach her again. But he didn't. And right after the next full moon she committed suicide. She left a note saying she couldn't live with what she had become. You see, not only had this monster bitten her, he had turned her and then just left her to fend for herself. She didn't understand what was happening. She must have thought she was going crazy.

"After that incident things escalated. There was a killing, sometimes two, every month. It made Jason so angry. He knew no one in his precinct would believe him if he explained who, or what, was actually committing the murders. They would have sent him for psychiatric treatment.

"The authorities were looking for an animal; we were the only ones who knew they should be looking for a human. So, Jason started going out every full moon and walking around Grant Park. He was sure he could catch the werewolf. After all, he understood exactly what the problem was while the other cops didn't. He thought that was enough to protect himself.

"The night Jason was killed I was on patrol in my precinct. I heard the report: an officer had been mauled by a dog. I knew who it was, who it had to be." Tears fell freely from Shannon's eyes as she spoke.

"I got there as quickly as I could. But by the time I got to the hospital, he was gone. They said he'd lost too much blood to survive. I guess that was better, you know? What if he had survived? He wouldn't have wanted to live that way, either."

Dave reached out to touch his partner on the shoulder. He wanted to hug her, to hold her. To make it all better. But she straightened and brushed his hand away—still Shannon the prickly, he thought—and took another deep breath.

"I can't," she said harshly. "You can't offer me sympathy. You can't. I'll fall apart if you do. You wanted to know; this is how I have to tell it." She put her hands on the steering wheel and stared straight ahead out the windshield, no longer even glancing at Dave.

"After Jason died, I just wanted to get away from Chicago, go someplace quiet where I wouldn't have to worry about werewolves and witches." Shannon laughed. "What a joke that was. I don't know why I chose Rivelou. There must be something here that attracts the paranormal."

Dave nodded his head but said nothing.

"Anyway, I thought I was joining a sleepy, small-town police force, but after a couple of months here it started again. There were reports of a stray dog being sighted. It was a nightmare. That's when I asked my brother to come down and investigate.

"At first, he didn't believe me when I told him it had to be the same wolf, the one who killed Jason. Why would the werewolf have moved here from Chicago? It seemed like too much of a coincidence. But then we found the evidence. The werewolf who killed Jason was definitely the same one who killed that man in Mitchell Park last September."

"Let me guess. The werewolf was Professor Alexander Fontaine, right?"

"Remember, I'm not supposed to admit that to anyone. You can't let anyone know that you know. Both Chief Anderson and Hank Bertrand have made that very, very clear."

"So, Fontaine is dead?"

"I didn't say that."

"You didn't have to. It was self-defense, you know. You had to kill him."

"You think I killed him?" Shannon gave an incredulous laugh. "I wanted to. For Jason, for the woman in Chicago, for everyone else he'd hurt. But he'd knocked me out and tied me up," she said bitterly. "If it weren't for Ana, Chris and I would both be dead now. She changed into a wolf and, well, Fontaine was no match for her."

"Ana Dugan killed Fontaine? I never would have believed it!" he said, astonishment in his voice. "The few times I've seen her she's seemed so quiet and well, mousy, I guess."

"She is not! She's a wonderful woman, and my brother is lucky to have found her!" Shannon sprang quickly to her friend's defense. "And if you ever tell anyone what I told you... well, power or no power, you don't mess with Hank Bertrand's granddaughter. You know that, right? You'd probably get dropped into the Rivelou River or something."

"Wow! So, the chief knows all this?"

"He knows about Fontaine. He was there that night.

Helped hide the mess. But I've never talked to him about my background."

Dave sighed. "Well, this doesn't clear up much of anything, you know, Shannon. It actually just makes it all that much messier. You have power, the chief obviously suspects that you have power, and unless you can prove where you were last night, you're going to be a suspect in a really gruesome murder case."

CHAPTER 5

Shannon sat and stared in astonishment. She was stunned. Nothing Dave said could have surprised her more than this. Or offended her more, either.

"They thi...think th...that I..." she stammered, incensed. She took a breath and started again. "Chief Anderson, Detective Abello, you! You all think that I could have committed murder. Not just any murder. The most gruesome murder you've ever *seen*? You think I could have mutilated someone and cut her heart out?" Her voice rose higher in indignation the longer she spoke.

"I don't," Dave said quickly, hoping to stem the tide of her anger.

Shannon gave him a skeptical look, but at least she quit yelling at him. "No, really. I don't! I swear. I never did." He knew he sounded lame, but he wanted to convince her. He wanted to tell her how much he admired her. That he'd asked to become her partner because he'd been intrigued by her aloofness... by her reputation as a good cop... by her blond curls and body that didn't quit... No, that was really not what he needed to say to her right now. He mentally shook himself. Shannon figuring out that he was attracted to her was not going to help the situation.

He tried again. "I didn't think you were a suspect before. And now, after what you've just told me about your mother and your husband... no, no way. I believe you. You couldn't be involved in these murders. But the other guys on the force, and the chief, don't know you like I do. And Shannon, you've made it really, really difficult for the people here at the department to get to know you."

Dave leaned forward staring intently at his partner to emphasize his words. "You're secretive. You don't mix with the rest of us on the force. Some of the other guys believe that you think you're too good for us. You're always talking about how much better it was in Chicago. That doesn't make you a suspect, exactly, but when the subject does come up, you haven't made any friends who are going to come to your defense, and it's not in your favor."

She didn't say anything for several moments, just stared at him with such hurt in her big blue eyes that he wanted to take her in his arms, hold her, and tell her he would make it all better. But that wasn't what she needed right now, so Dave clenched his fists and stared back at her.

Finally, she responded. "So let me make sure I understand you," she began, speaking slowly and carefully. "You are saying that just because I don't open up and spill my guts to everyone I meet I'm a suspect in a murder case?"

Her voice was low, quiet; she was trying hard to sound icy and cold, but he could hear the pain behind it. David winced. Her obvious hurt was worse somehow than her earlier anger.

"No. Not because you don't 'spill your guts' to everyone. Because you have power and you haven't been honest about it. The chief's given you every opportunity to tell him about your powers. I've heard him."

"When has he...? Ohh," she said in a long breath as she remembered several conversations she'd had with the chief after the Alexander Fontaine affair. "That's what he was trying to say. I guess I really was clueless. I thought he was trying to tell me not to mention anything about Hank Bertrand and the other shapeshifters to anyone. It never occurred to me he was asking about me, and my power."

Dave shook his head in frustration. "You've been so busy denying that you have power that you didn't listen to what he was really saying. And by the way, you should know that Hank Bertrand is the only one who's been on your side. If he wasn't vouching for you, you'd have been brought in for questioning after the second murder."

Shannon shook her head in disgust. She seemed to have forgotten her hurt, Dave noticed with relief. Anger he could handle, but when she looked at him with those baby blue eyes so full of shadows and sorrow, he just wanted to take her in his arms, kiss her, and make it all better.

He shook his head slightly. Now was not the time to be thinking about how attracted he was to his beautiful but very prickly partner. Maybe, after today she would at least start seeing him as a friend—something she really needed right about now whether she acknowledged it or not. Yes, anything more than friendship would have to wait until after they got this mess sorted out, he told himself sternly. He realized that Shannon had been talking, or to be more accurate ranting, for the last few minutes and he hadn't even heard a word she said.

"...Hank Bertrand! I wish my brother had never gotten mixed up with these people. I wish I'd never seen this place. Hank Bertrand has too damn much influence in this town."

"Yeah, maybe so. There are a lot of witches in my coven who think he has too much influence, too. But he's kept this town off the map for decades, and he keeps us safe—not just the shapeshifters but everyone with paranormal talents. He's a big influence in this community—with everyone who has power here. And whether they know it or not, he helps the people who live here who don't have any power, also."

His voice took on an edge. If Shannon didn't wake up soon and realize just how things worked in this town, she was going to be in big trouble. "You wanted to come to a town that was safe. Hank Bertrand is one of the reasons why it is a haven for people like us. Yeah, he can be a bit dictatorial. And yeah, maybe we're a little clannish here. But it's been a good, *safe* place for people to live—people with power and people without—for years. Until now, that is.

"Now, someone is out there breaking the rules. Rules that have kept us secure and under the radar. Someone is killing people and making it look like witches are doing it. I want to find out who it is—before they hurt someone else. I know it's no one from my own coven."

Shannon didn't like Dave's tone. He said he believed her, but did he really? "Are you so sure about that?" she said with all the sarcasm she could muster. "Are you so sure one of your own hasn't gone off the reservation?"

"Yeah, I'm sure. Because if they had they would have done it right. Like I said before, whoever is involved here doesn't know what they are doing."

"But I've been trained."

"So you say. But no one here knows that. We don't know your background; we don't know what kind of training you have had. You haven't let us know about it. But more importantly, you haven't let us know you!"

Shannon sighed and let go of her anger. He was right, damn it. "So what do you think I should do?" she asked.

Dave let out a breath of relief. He hadn't been sure she'd listen to him, and even if she did, he'd been afraid she was just stubborn enough to try to go it her own way and not let him help her.

"Go talk to the Chief," he said urgently. "Tell him everything you've told me. Go to him now before he sends someone to talk to you."

"Will you go with me?" He heard the fear in her voice. It was the first time since he'd known her, he thought, that he had ever seen Shannon Kelly the least bit vulnerable.

"Of course. End of shift."

"End of shift?" she repeated with a grimace, and a question in her voice. She'd really like to put this off indefinitely. "Yeah, end of shift," she said again more definitely. Now that she had finally acknowledged something she'd been hiding for years, she figured she'd better face it before she lost her courage.

"End of shift," Dave said with a smile, holding out his hand and they shook on it.

Shannon started the car, radioed that they were off their break, and headed out of the parking lot and back on patrol.

CHAPTER 6

The rest of day continued with the usual series of minor alarms, burglaries, fender benders, and neighbor disputes that kept the pair running from one call to another, with little chance to talk again. When they finally returned to the station to type up their reports, Shannon's desire to just get it over and talk with the chief as soon as possible had dimmed.

She began to hope that the chief would be too busy to see her. She hoped that Dave would forget. She hoped for lightning to strike her and make talking to the chief unnecessary. But luck was not on her side. Dave had poked his head into Chief Anderson's office as soon as they got in and made sure that he knew they wanted to talk to him.

As soon as their reports were finished, Dave turned to her. "Ready?" he asked.

She took a deep breath. "As I'll ever be," she said with a grimace. She headed for the chief's office with Dave right behind her and knocked on the door.

"Come in."

Chief Anderson was a fit man in his late 50's, tall, dark-skinned, with a deep, booming voice. His size had intimidated many a criminal. Some of the cops under him swore it was his size alone that accounted for the tons of arrests he had to his record. Others, those on the force who knew more, whispered that his power came from another, more unusual source.

His mother had been a siren. And while his father was a witch from the island of Jamaica, he had inherited only his mother's power, not his father's. He was a rare and unusual creature: a male siren. His power was in his voice. With it he could compel people. It was said he could make a person do whatever he wanted them to do, for good or evil. Luckily, Anderson had a strict code of honor, and while he had on occasion been known to compel criminals to tell the truth about their crimes, he had never used his power for evil.

Dave knew that the chief could have used his power to force Shannon to talk to him. She wouldn't have realized what was being done to her. He also knew that the chief did not treat his cops, or anyone else, that way unless it was an absolute necessity.

Now, Shannon stood in front of him, nervously wringing her left hand with her right. "I understand I need to tell you some things about my background," she said in a low voice.

"Sit down, Officer Kelly. You too, Officer Thorne. I assume you've asked him to stay?" the chief said to her, acknowledging the fact that David still stood right behind her, his hand hovering supportively near her back, as if he wanted to pat her, but was afraid to.

"Yes. He's the one who convinced me I needed to talk to you," she said, taking one of the two straight-backed chairs that faced the chief's desk. People had heard him say it was no accident that his "guest" chairs weren't very welcoming. It kept unwanted visitors from taking up too much time chatting in his office. Shannon found the hard, straight surface a comfort now. It forced her to sit up straight and look the chief in the eye, A fact she hoped increased her air of sincerity.

"Dave's the reason I'm here, and he knows all about what I need to tell you. I just told him this morning," she added quickly, afraid that the chief might think her partner had been hiding things from him.

The chief nodded as Dave took a seat next to her. He started to reach his hand out to her, but Shannon noticed the gesture and shook her head minutely. She might want his moral support, but anything more would be too much right now.

The silence stretched on until the chief finally said, "So, what would you like to tell me?"

"I never thought I'd have to talk about this. I thought it was all behind me." She stopped, hearing the defensive tone in her voice, took a deep breath and tried again.

"I mean it's not on any job application form I've ever seen. 'Do you have paranormal abilities? Do you belong to a coven? Are you a good witch or a bad witch?'" she quoted, unable to keep the rising sarcasm out of her voice.

From the corner of her eye she saw Dave raise his fist to his mouth to hide a grin.

"I'll grant you that, Officer Kelly," the chief said, and she noticed that his lips were twitching. She felt relieved. Maybe this wouldn't be as bad as she had thought.

"I may have to have a discussion with HR on whether or not it is a violation of any discrimination policies if we add some of those questions to our hiring applications," he said dryly. "But frankly, the subject has never come up before. When I interviewed you for the position, I noticed your power. I assumed you felt the same thing and were just being polite in not mentioning it. That you would bring it up once you were on the force.

"Then, a few months later your brother moved here. It was very well known that he was a Hunter. There was some concern, but Hank Bertrand has vouched for him, and I've spoken with Chris personally."

"He didn't tell you anything about me—or our background. He would have told me if he had," Shannon interrupted.

"No, no. I don't want you to think your brother was gossiping about you," Anderson assured her. "I wouldn't have asked him to discuss you. I expected you to come to me yourself," he said with just a hint of rebuke. He gave her a moment to let that sink in before continuing.

"As I was saying, your brother and I have come to an understanding. He will not interfere in this department although occasionally there may be cases where, legally, we are unable to act and we may have to call on his—unique talents—if, and only if, the case involves a paranormal, either as the victim or as a suspect.

"I thought at that time that you, too, would come to speak with me, but you did not. I've tried to respect your privacy, but with everything that has happened, I expected you to talk with me well before this. The other members of the force who have power have already come in and discussed things with me. They made sure that they were in the clear on both the murders that occurred before this morning. But you never did. It puts you in a bad light."

Shannon took a deep breath. "My mother was a witch. Her

name was Beatrix Callich Spier. She taught me... well... everything she knew. And yes, she was dark. She did things... evil things... I never wanted to be like that."

As Shannon stuttered through the same explanation she had earlier given to Dave, she began to feel lighter, somehow. Less burdened. These two men knew the kind of power she had and how she had been trained. They understood the choices she had made. And she could see in their eyes that they approved.

"Yes, under the circumstances, I can understand your reluctance to use your power, or even to acknowledge it, Officer Kelly," the chief began. Shannon could tell by the look on his face, though, that the rest of what he was about to say was not going to go down so easily.

"Your mother was well-known before she disappeared about ten years ago."

The question in his voice invited her to comment about her mother's disappearance. That was something she'd never do. After a moment or two of silence as she refused to acknowledge her chief's curiosity, he continued.

"But right now, we have to put some other matters to rest. Where, exactly, were you last night?"

"I was home alone."

"The whole night? Your brother wasn't there? You didn't see him or his fiancée?"

This statement really got Shannon's dander up in the way the question about her mother had not. "I am so tired of being tied to the Bertrand clan," she spat out. "Are they so important that if they vouch for my movements I'm okay—and if they can't I'm a damned suspect?"

"You don't have to like it, Officer Kelly, but that is the way things stand right now," the chief said coldly. "You don't have anyone who can vouch for your movements. You've now told me enough about your background that I am inclined to believe you could not have done these murders..."

"Sir, you could..." began Dave, but the chief cut him off with a quick motion of his hand.

"I know what you are thinking, but I don't believe that is a good idea right now. Officer Kelly needs to learn to trust us, and

I don't think that would be the way to go about it."

Shannon looked back and forth at the two men, a question in her eyes as she tried to understand the cryptic comments passing between them.

"What are you talking about? Is there a way that you would be sure I didn't do these murders?"

The chief ran his hand over his face. "Yes, you know there are paranormal ways to compel you to tell the truth, and I, in particular, am an expert at them. While using my ability might convince the members of the force who have power that you were innocent, the evidence wouldn't stand up in a court of law. And there are others in the town who do not have power but still tend to look askance at any newcomers. Talk could spread and it wouldn't be good. While Rivelou is a nexus that attracts many people of power, we learned many centuries ago that those powers cannot be used instead of the laws of the country."

"Witch trials? The Inquisition? Don't you think we are a little beyond that?" she asked sarcastically.

"As paranormals we live in the shadows. You know *that;* you've lived it. The way we survive is to keep the world at large unaware that we exist. The media has linked the three deaths and is calling them 'The Artificial Witch Slayings.' The name they've chosen shows just how much the people in this town— paranormal or non-para—are aware of things.

"It's hitting a lot closer to home than we'd like the non-para media to be. It's getting more and more difficult these days to stay in the shadows. But that's a discussion for another time. For now, Officer Kelly, let me just say that while I believe in your innocence, there are a number of people on this force who need to be convinced.

"I suggest that you go back to the other murders and see if you have an alibi for either of those dates. That would go a long way to relieving the suspicion. And for now, I also suggest that you mind your p's and q's. You're both dismissed."

The chief pointedly picked up some papers on his desk and began to go through them, making it clear that the interview was over.

"Wow. That didn't go as well as I hoped," Shannon said as

they headed to the locker room to change out of their uniforms and head home for the day.

"Shannon, I'm really sorry. I thought he would be more sympathetic."

"No, he's right. You believe me, and maybe even he really believes me, but there are a lot of other people I'm going to have to convince. Dammit! I knew it. Any time I get involved with anything to do with witchcraft things go badly for me. I just need to stay the hell away from all of it." She scowled at him.

"Maybe instead you should learn a little more about it. What your mother taught you was only one side of it. Let me show you that not everything—or everyone—with power is evil."

"No." she said definitely and headed out to the parking lot. But Dave pursued her to the door of her Kia Soul.

"Think about it," he said, leaning on her door.

"I have. No." She yanked the door out from under him, making him stumble a little.

She saw him in the rearview mirror as she drove out of the parking lot. He just stood there, shaking his head at her.

CHAPTER 7

Shannon decided to stop at the small grocery store near her house on her way home. After the day that she had just had, she figured pampering herself with a cold beer and a steak on the grill was in order. She passed the campus and watched frisbee players and sunbathers out enjoying the weather. She tried to remember when she had been that carefree. When she'd been married to Jason, they had spent weekends doing "normal" things—going to movies, just spending time with friends. Now it seemed like another world—one she could never find again.

Next door to the grocery, which stood in a small strip mall a few blocks from the campus, was The Wolf's Den. It was a cute boutique that catered to the college kids but also carried clothing that someone a mature 33 years of age could appreciate. The store was run by Abigail Mohr, who had become a good friend of Shannon's.

Abigail was a native of Rivelou but didn't seem as clannish as many of the residents Shannon had met so far. Like the other cops, Shannon thought, even though she now had an explanation for some of their reserve. Unlike most of the other Rivelou natives, Abigail had always made Shannon feel welcome.

After stowing her groceries in the car, Shannon stopped to admire the new window display at the boutique. The cute, stuffed wolf puppies were placed as if they were picnicking with a basket of the various delicacies the boutique offered: expensive cheeses, jams and jellies from Europe, fancy crackers. It made an engaging display.

"Wolf. Duh. Never realized before just why the university's mascot is a wolf," she thought. Supposedly it was because wolves were native to the area and had been found in abundance back in the early 1800s when Rivelou was settled. Now, Shannon realized the joke that the residents with paranormal abilities had played on their less-gifted neighbors.

The wolf in the mascot logo, displayed on some sweatshirts and other clothing she could see on a rack in the store, looked suspiciously vicious and hungry, and maybe just a little like a werewolf.

She entered the store and found there was a new clerk.

"Hi, can I help you?" the perky teen asked.

"Is Abby here?"

"Yes, she's in the back, unpacking some new merchandise. Can I get her for you?"

"Yes, please. Just tell her Shannon is here, and I want to see if she's interested in beer and steak tonight."

The girl grinned. "Well, if she's not, I'll be your new friend. I'm Winnie by the way. Winnie Thorne."

"Wait. You're Dave's cousin, right?"

"Yep. You got me."

"He's my partner."

"Ohh. You're that Shannon." The girl's face turned red. "I'll just go get Abigail." She hurried into the back room.

Well, that went well. Thought Dave said he hadn't talked about me.

A moment later Abby came out of the back room, wiping her face. "It's damn hot back there today, but I have to unpack the new merchandise," she said. "What's up with you? According to the news it's been a bad day for the cops in town."

"A worse day for the girl who was killed," Shannon said.

"Oh God, I didn't mean it to sound that way, Shannon."

"No, I think I'm just taking everything everyone says the wrong way right now. It's been a hell of a day. I was wondering if you wanted to come by my house for a brew and a steak."

"I'd love to. Can you give me a half hour to clean up here? Winnie?" She turned to the girl who was standing behind the counter trying to pretend she wasn't listening. "We've gone over the closing procedures. Do you think you're ready to do it by yourself?

"Of course. I'd love to do it."

Abby laughed. "You say that now. Let's see how you feel about staying late in a couple of months when it isn't so new and exciting."

She turned back to Shannon. "Look, just let me finish a couple of things. Did you see the new store two doors down? Go browse, and I'll meet you there in a few."

Baubles and Beads was the name of the new boutique. It carried an eclectic mix of jewelry, crystals, bath items, books, and handcrafted clothes that looked like they came straight out of a 1975 hippie store.

Chimes jingled when she entered the shop, and her nose was assaulted by the smell of patchouli incense. As she browsed the assortment of inexpensive necklaces and earrings, a woman glided silently over to her, startling Shannon with her quiet approach.

"Good afternoon, I'm Salvia," she said.

"Oh, sorry, I guess I'm just jumpy this afternoon. You have a lot of nice things."

"Yes, I can see your spirit is agitated," the woman said, folding her hands in front of her and working on looking wise and serene. She was dressed in a black and white caftan with a vaguely African print. Her long hair was too black not to have come from a bottle. It looked as if she had ironed it to make it that straight. Heavy make-up coated her eyes. If it had been October instead of May, Shannon would have thought she was dressed in a Morticia Addams costume.

"I've got several crystals, incense, and other items to help bring you tranquility," the woman continued.

Was it possible to smile and roll your eyes at the same time? Shannon hoped the eye roll wasn't noticeable as she tried for a politely interested look. She had been totally clueless to all the paranormal vibes in this town until Dave opened her eyes this morning. She'd assumed her brother Chris meeting Ana and the wolf pack was a result of the search for her husband's killer. Now it seemed that everyone in the town had some connection to the paranormal, from Abigail's wolf cub display in her store window to the overdone mystical vibe in this new shop.

She realized Salvia was still looking at her hopefully, wanting to make a sale. Of course she did; the store was brand new, and the woman probably needed the money. But Shannon wasn't going to fall for the "your spirit is disturbed" bullshit so easily.

She'd ignored her own training in witchcraft for a long time, but she still remembered some of the basics. And something soothing would be nice after the day she'd had. She didn't think it would take any great power to notice that she looked hot, sweaty, and agitated.

"You don't have any bergamot essential oil by any chance?" she asked. She chose an herb she knew was soothing, but not the most common, lavender, just to see what the store owner would say.

"Of course; we also have a lovely line of soaps and bath salts that will help to ease your stress. They are right over here."

Shannon followed Salvia to the left side of the shop where various bath items were displayed on shelves alongside small soap dishes and incense holders decorated with stars, moons, trees, and other nature symbols. It was all very tasteful and if it hadn't been for her conversations with Dave and Chief Anderson, she might not have picked up on the subtle paranormal vibe of the display.

"Hey, Babe, where did you go? I could use a little help back here." They heard a voice from the back room calling.

"Pardon me. That's my partner calling. I need to see what he wants."

Shannon turned as a man came out of the back room.

He was large and muscular. His well-defined arms and chest stretched his black t-shirt. It also showed off the sleeve of tattoos that decorated his left arm. The intricate pattern drew her eye, but she didn't want to seem to be ogling the man.

"Harrison, we have a customer," Salvia said.

Again, Shannon almost snorted. The man's parents could not have known he'd grow up to be about six foot three, muscular, with a heavy, dark beard and decorated with enough tattoos to suggest he was part of a biker gang. No one could look less like a "Harrison" than this man.

"Oh, sorry. Hey, don't let me stop you from shopping," he said to her briefly, then turned back to Salvia.

"Babe, can I have just a minute back here? I need to know what you want to do with some of the things from last night."

Salvia followed him into the back, and Shannon heard a whispered conversation but couldn't make out any words. She could tell from the tone, however, that the two were not pleased with each other at the moment.

"I've got to get back out front. You just deal with it however you want," she heard Salvia say right before she reentered the store.

"I'm so sorry. Getting the store open means there are a million questions to be answered, and every time one gets solved, two more pop up," she said to Shannon.

"Maybe you need the bergamot more than I do," Shannon said.

"Or a giant margarita," Salvia mumbled, turning away to smooth down her long, sleek hair and plaster her serene expression back on.

Shannon hid her smile. She wasn't sure the woman had really intended her to hear that.

"Now, where were we? Oh yes, the bergamot is always a good choice for relaxation. Have you ever tried chanting while you use your essential oils?"

Shannon didn't try to disguise her eye roll this time.

"I see you are not a believer."

"A believer in what?" She knew very well where this conversation was going but wanted to see exactly what approach Salvia would take. Before this morning, she would have totally discounted the possibility that the shopkeeper had any power. But now, Shannon wasn't so sure; she hadn't used her own magic in so long it was difficult to pick up the subtle aura of power that surrounded most paranormals. Was the woman a witch or not? *Are you a good witch or a bad witch?* The line flickered through her mind. She shook it off. Salvia was doing her best to be charming and make a sale that was probably badly needed since the store had just opened.

She let herself be led around the shelves, looking at a variety of items she remembered from her childhood: candles in a variety of colors, feathers, bundles of herbs. Crystals were displayed prettily in copper bowls of various sizes. They ended the tour at a shelf which featured tarot cards and Ouija boards as well as pamphlets and books. She found herself drawn to one, *Witchcraft: A Guide for Beginners.* She picked it up and began leafing through it.

"That's a very good book for beginners," Salvia said, noticing her interest. "It gives you a good overview of the history of Wiccans as well as some beginning witchcraft spells."

Shannon didn't bother to correct the woman on the difference between witches and Wiccans. Witches practiced magic. Wiccans followed the Wiccan religion, which included some magic. While Wiccans were witches, not all witches were Wiccans. But Salvia seemed so open and naïve in her desire to help Shannon. The book probably had nothing to offer her, but in light of the woman's friendliness and obvious desire to be helpful—not to mention Dave's suggestion she start to relearn some of her skills—she decided to buy it.

Salvia clapped her hands delightedly. "I know you'll enjoy it."

At that moment, Harrison walked back into the room.

"Harrison, I think we have a convert." Salvia turned to him and said.

"Oh, are you interested in witchcraft?" He put his arm around Salvia and drew her to him. "Babe, I told you this town would be good for us." He gave her a kiss on the forehead.

"Yes, you were right." She returned his kiss with one of her own, then turned again to Shannon.

"Harrison sees things, you know," she said in a confidential tone.

"Babe," he said deprecatingly. "Don't put it like that. I just get feelings sometimes."

"If he tells you he has a feeling, don't ignore him. He doesn't like to admit it, but he can see the future."

Shannon smiled uncomfortably and tried to hurry the purchase along. While the pair seemed harmless and friendly, they were also just a bit eccentric, and the whole thing was becoming uncomfortable. Luckily, at that moment the door chimes jingled again, and Abby walked in.

"Hey, Shannon, are you ready to go?"

"I'm just paying now," she replied.

"Oh Abigail, are you the one who sent Shannon to us?"

The use of her name startled Shannon. She hadn't given the woman her name. Of course, she realized quickly, Abigail had just mentioned it. Still, somehow it felt uncomfortably intimate coming from Saliva, as if they were friends instead of having just met.

Shannon handed over her bank card, and Salvia wrapped the oil carefully so it wouldn't break and handed her a bag with her purchases.

"I hope you'll be us visiting again," Harrison said, giving her a long, penetrating look before taking her hand for a moment. "In fact, I'm sure you will be."

When Salvia gave him an angry look, he quickly dropped Shannon's hand and walked into the back room.

"Well, that was really odd," Shannon said as they got into her car.

"Yeah, they are a little weird at times, but they do seem friendly. There's no harm in them; they're interested in healing and spirituality. It's a good thing," said Abigail. "We can all use that sometimes. Now let's go relax and eat those steaks."

CHAPTER 8

Shannon and Abby brought their salad and beers to the backyard so Shannon could put the steaks on the grill and keep an eye on them. The old Victorian house on Westbridge Street that Shannon had purchased when she moved to town still need a lot of work. She had already restored the kitchen and living room, and her bedroom and bathroom had been completed, but there were several other rooms that still needed work. The room Chris had slept in until he moved in with Ana was badly in need of some plaster work and a coat of paint. That's what Shannon hoped to work on this weekend while she was off.

"So, what did you think of my new neighbors over at the shop?" Abby asked, taking a sip of her beer.

"Well… the store is interesting, a lot of nice things in it."

"What did you buy?"

Shannon didn't want to admit that she had purchased a book on witchcraft. "Oh, just a few things…"

"Did you get any jewelry? She has a lot of pretty necklaces and bracelets."

"No." Shannon started to move the bag off the kitchen table.

"You're intriguing me now," laughed Abby. "I've got to see what you're hiding." She put a hand on the paper bag, stopping Shannon from moving it.

"Abby, really."

"Hmm, feels like a book. She didn't get you to buy one of those books on witchcraft, did she?"

Shannon turned red. "Well, I felt sorry for them. They're opening a new store and obviously need sales. I just wanted to help them out," she stammered.

"Really, Shannon. Of all the things in the store! If you actually want to know more about the craft, you could just ask me. Or Dave of course. No use spending money on a book that might be filled with bad information when you have teachers right at hand."

Shannon gaped at her. "Y…you too?" she stammered.

"What? You didn't know? You can't feel my power, my aura?"

Shannon raised her eyes to the ceiling. "No! No more. I can't take any more today." To her horror tears flowed down her cheeks. She sniffed and wiped her nose with the back of her hand. "Now look what you've made me do."

"Shannon, I'm so sorry. I didn't mean to make you cry." Abby walked over and gave her a quick hug. "Dave called me earlier to tell me a little bit about what's been happening. He said you'd talked with the chief. He figured you might need to open up to a friend."

"He told you? He told you what the chief thinks?"

"All he said was he thought you might need someone to talk to. I don't know anything more than that. Then when you stopped by the shop and asked me for dinner, I figured he was right. That's why you were there; you were ready to talk about being a witch."

"Well, with everything that went on today I hate to say it, but he's probably right. I could use someone to talk to about it all. On the being a witch part… I'm not sure I'll ever be ready. I do know I don't want to think about it for a while. Can we just eat dinner first without talking about anything serious?"

"Of course. I'll get the salad," Abby stood up. You pull the steaks off the grill."

They decided to eat in the garden. Now that the sun was going down, things had cooled off a bit, and the temperature was pleasant outside.

The rickety wrought iron table and chairs had been left in the yard by the last owner. Shannon planned to repair and paint them this summer. When she had time. For now, they would do even if the table tended to slant a little and the chairs were wobbly.

Shannon turned on the star-shaped string of party lights her brother had helped her hang from the edge of the porch to the big oak tree. The tree was filled with the tiny new leaves of spring, making a pretty picture in the dusk.

When she had moved into the old home last year, it had been more important to work on the interior of the house. The backyard was still a mess. This summer she planned to turn the overgrown beds and untrimmed bushes into a delightful respite. For now, the growing dusk and the twinkling lights hid the weeds and the messy, leaf-filled beds, turning the garden into exactly what she was hoping it would become—a quiet oasis to sit and relax.

The conversation stayed neutral through dinner, but when they were back in the kitchen cleaning up the dishes, Abby brought the subject up again.

"So, you know I'm a witch, right?"

"Not until you told me tonight, no."

"You can't feel my power?"

"No, just like I told Dave, I've tried to cut all that out of my life. I haven't practiced or used any of my powers since I got out of high school. I hoped any power I did have would just go away. And maybe it has since everyone is talking to me about sensing things that I'm just not noticing."

"You know blocking it won't make you lose it. It doesn't work like that. Your powers may be rusty, and the channels barred, but they're all still there whenever you're ready to pick them up again."

"What if I'm never ready?" Shannon said angrily. "What if I never want to use it? I feel like you and Dave and the chief are forcing me to do something and be something I swore I'd never do or be again."

"You know your power isn't good or evil, don't you, Shannon? It's how you use it, right?"

"So you and Dave say."

"Let me tell you my family's story. Then maybe you'll understand a little more."

"Well, if I have to listen, I think I'm going to need another beer," Shannon said. "You want one?" she asked rather ungraciously as she opened the refrigerator.

"Sure. It's a long story. Let's take this back outside and get comfortable. Now that the sun is down, I think it's cooler out there than in here. You are seriously going to want to consider

AC this summer. It can be brutal here."

Shannon snagged a bag of chips, and they headed back out to the garden and settled at the table again. "I'm going to get some more comfortable lounge chairs as soon as they go on sale," Shannon started, hoping to derail the conversation.

"I'm sure it will be lovely. You have great taste, Shannon. But back to my story." Abby firmly took the conversation back to the topic at hand.

"I'm named for my six times great-grandmother, Abigail Barker."

"Wait. Wasn't she…?"

"I'm glad to see you do know a little of the history of witchcraft in the United States. Yes, Abigail Barker was one of the people accused at the Salem Witch trials.

"She was born in Massachusetts and married a man named Ebenezer Barker. They both had power, and they both used it for good—they were not evil witches. Of course, they practiced very quietly at the time—as history has shown, it wasn't a popular era for people to advertise that they were witches.

"Anyway, Abigail and Ebenezer were living in Andover, Massachusetts, and had three children when the famous witch hysteria started. A number of family members were accused of witchcraft. Ebenezer's brother-in-law and his brother-in-law's mother, his brother William, and a niece and nephew were all imprisoned.

"You know how these kinds of rumors feed on themselves—we see them even today with social media conspiracies."

Shannon nodded. "I can't tell you the number of times I've been called to a home or business because rumors are being spread. It's usually someone deciding their neighbor is dealing drugs or something like that rather than witchcraft, but the principle's the same. It's mostly because they just don't like their neighbors."

"And remember that whole thing about the pizza place in Washington D.C. that was supposedly kidnapping children and selling them for devil worship? The Witch Trials were essentially the same thing."

Shannon nodded her head. She opened the bag of chips she had brought out and set them in the middle of the table where Abby could reach them also. This sounded like it was going to be a very long story.

"When Abigail was accused and jailed, Ebenezer joined the resistance and signed petitions to free the accused. I'm pretty proud of Ebenezer. Yeah, he was a witch, too, and yeah, there were certainly men being accused, but not nearly as many men as women, and I'm sure there were plenty of husbands who disavowed their wives or just went into hiding, whether they had power, or believed, or not. Ebenezer didn't do that. He stood up for his wife and family."

"Sounds like he was a good guy," Shannon said, pushing the bag of chips toward Abby, who took a handful.

"Well, anyway, the petitions didn't work. Abigail was indicted for witchcraft. After several months in jail, she was put on trial, and she was found innocent. I don't remember the details; I imagine the fires of hysteria were blowing themselves out by that time. At any rate, Abigail was released and went home to her husband and children. She died peacefully of old age. Her children had children—there are a lot of descendants, though not all of us have power, or even acknowledge the truth that the family members actually were witches."

"Bet that makes for some interesting family reunions," Shannon said.

"Oh, believe it. And some of that friction is why in the mid-1800s my branch of the family headed west and settled here."

"Well, that brings me to the next question. Why Rivelou? Why are there so many paranormals here?"

"You know about ley lines, right?"

"Of course. They're imaginary lines drawn by humans between various natural landmarks, like rivers or mountains, and ancient sites. They're completely manmade. There's nothing magical about them. No one even thought them up until the early 1900s."

Abby rubbed the back of her neck and looked at the

ceiling for a few moments. "You really have had a number done on you, haven't you? Your power is real, whether you acknowledge it or not. And yes, the concept of ley lines became known to the non-para world in the twentieth century; that's when they became popular in novels and movies. That doesn't mean they didn't exist before that. And between the ancient mounds of the Native Americans, several other ancient locations in the area, and our position in this protected horseshoe bend in the river, Rivelou is at the nexus of several ley lines."

As Shannon was about to refute everything Abby had just said, she heard the back door open.

CHAPTER 9

"Hey, here you are," her brother Chris said, coming into the backyard with his fiancée, Ana, and soon to be step-daughter, Sophie.

"Hey guys, I didn't expect you tonight," Shannon said as Sophie and Ana sat down and made themselves comfortable in the two extra chairs.

"Sophie's not going over to her dad's until Sunday. Melanie had the baby this afternoon, and they're keeping both of them at the hospital until then," Ana said, referring to Sophie's stepmother. "It's a baby boy, and Jonathan is thrilled to the moon and back. He wants to spend tomorrow at the hospital with them."

"Yeah, Dad was a little over the top when he came by this afternoon," Sophie said with a smile. "I'll get to see my new brother on Sunday."

Shannon was glad to see how obviously happy the girl was about her new brother. She exchanged looks with Ana. It was well-known that Jonathan was rather self-centered and already didn't pay as much attention to his daughter as Ana thought he should. She hoped he didn't ignore Sophie in favor of the new baby. Thankfully that wasn't her worry. She had enough on her own plate right now.

"And that means she can help me with painting the bedroom over here," Ana added.

Sophie made a face.

"Don't worry; you'll still have time with your friends, but we're going to get that back bedroom painted for Shannon first," she told her daughter. "That's why we stopped by tonight. I want to take a look at the room, see how much paint we think we'll need, and make a final decision on the color you want. That way I can get it picked up first thing in the morning and start on the project as soon as possible."

"Great! I'll head right up with you, and we can take a look." Shannon hopped up from her seat so fast she almost spilled the can of beer she had been nursing.

"Oops," Ana said, grabbing the can before the contents spilled. "I can take a look by myself. I don't want to disturb you."

"She's just trying to get out of the conversation we were having," Abby said.

"Tattletale," Shannon muttered.

"What conversation?" Chris asked.

"We were talking about why there are so many paranormals in the area, and I was explaining ley lines and the nexus we live in to her."

"You got my sister to talk about something paranormal! What did you do? Hold her down? She never even wants to admit anything paranormal exists."

"Should we really be having this conversation in front of Sophie?" Shannon said in an effort to get everyone off the subject once again.

"I'm fourteen, not eight, Shannon. I know all about ley lines. Hey, I'm a werewolf, remember. I changed for the first time last month."

"You're no help, Kid," Shannon grumbled.

"So, what got you talking about this now?" Ana asked. Obviously, the painting project was going to be put off until everyone had a chance to put their two cents in on why she didn't want anything to do with the paranormal. But there were some things she just couldn't talk about. She'd told Dave far more than she had planned to this morning. It was enough for one day. There were still things she'd never shared with anyone but Jason, things she hadn't even talked about with her brother.

"It's work," she said.

"You mean The Artificial Witch Murders. There was a third one this morning, Ana; I don't know if you heard. Chief Anderson called me in to talk about it," said Chris. He grabbed a few chips, sat down in one of the chairs, and scooped Ana into his lap. She put her arm around him and stole a few of his chips.

"The chief talked to you?" Shannon almost squeaked. "What did he say? Did he say anything about me?"

"Why would he say anything about you to Chris?" Ana asked.

"Because she hasn't wanted to admit that she's a witch," Chris said.

"I thought everyone knew she was a witch. You can just tell," Sophie said.

"Sophie, a little tact, please. Shannon doesn't practice witchcraft and doesn't…"

"Want to admit she's a witch," finished Abby.

"Hey, I'm right here guys." Shannon pointed at herself. "Don't have to talk about me as if I'm not." It did no good.

"What does Shannon not admitting she's a witch have to do with these murders?" added Abby. "Yeah, I heard a body was found this morning out by the Mounds, but I didn't know it was related to any of the earlier killings."

"I've admitted it to practically the whole damn town today," Shannon complained. "And the chief specifically said we were not to talk about the murders with anyone outside the department. Which brings me back to why he was discussing it with you, Chris."

"It's the whole nature of the murders. He wanted to know if I'd seen anything like it before. Some of the ritual markings that they found look similar to Wiccan symbols, but they aren't quite right. I think he talked with your partner about that, too. The chief thought maybe I knew of some coven or other group that used something similar."

Chris was well known as a Hunter who searched out paranormal creatures that broke the laws of their pack or coven. In the past few months, his role as a Hunter had morphed into unofficial "police/enforcer" of paranormals in the area. He was working with Chief Anderson to gain more acceptance of this role with the packs and covens. Now, he looked toward Sophie as he mentioned "markings." Yes, she was fourteen, as she had just reminded them, but she didn't need to hear all of the gruesome details of these murders.

Her mother took the hint. "Sophie, let's go up and look at that bedroom. You can pick the color."

"But Mom, I want to hear…"

"Sophie, upstairs with me right now, or we are heading home."

"Yes, Mom. I can just look it up on PackNet anyway," she said, referring to the private "dark web" where paranormals of all types could exchange information safely. Ana's grandfather Hank Bertrand had spearheaded its development in the past several years. Dragging her feet as slowly as she could, Sophie followed her mother into the house.

"Look Shannon, I've already told them there is no way you are involved," Chris said as soon as the door closed.

"Damn it, I hate that they take your word over mine. I'm the cop here, not you."

"Why would anyone think Shannon is involved? Everyone who knows her…"

"That's just it, Abby, apparently my fellow cops think I'm standoffish and snobby, and that makes me a murder suspect." She tried to hide the hurt in her voice, but evidently her brother and best friend knew her too well. Abby reached over and took her hand reassuringly.

"The easiest thing to do is to give them an alibi," Chris said.

"Well, that would be easy if I had one. I was on duty for the February murder, but these last two I was home alone."

"Damn it, I should never have moved in with Ana and left you alone. If I'd been here…"

"That's just silly, Chris." Shannon reached over and patted his arm. "You're marrying Ana and should be with her. And I don't need a 24/7 babysitter."

"On TV they always say if someone has an alibi for one murder, it's obvious they can't have committed the others. Doesn't your having an alibi for one of the nights clear you?" asked Abby.

"Well, usually that would be true. In this case, though, it looks like several people may have been involved. Shannon could have missed one night but been there for the others," Chris said.

"And that means that we either figure out who did this, or I'm the police department's prime suspect."

"I think we may need to call in the big guns on this," Chris said, getting up and beginning to pace.

"What does that mean?" asked Abby.

"We're going to have to talk to Hank Bertrand. He's the alpha of the shapeshifters, and he wields a lot of influence with the other paranormals in the area."

"I don't know if that's such a good idea," Abby said. "This is not shapeshifter business—it's for the coven to deal with."

"No! No! No!" shouted Shannon. "I am a cop; I will deal with this through legal, non-para means. I don't need any more paranormal involvement—not Hank Bertrand, not PackNet, and certainly not the leader of a coven."

"But you do, Honey," her brother. "You have to admit that these murders have to do with the paranormal, whether the people involved have powers or whether they are just wannabes. Abby's right. We need to talk to both Cassandra and to Hank."

Shannon rolled her eyes. They wanted her to discuss why she didn't want to use her powers with the Alpha shifter and the local High Priestess. She'd been hiding secrets for a long time; what if they could see through her layers of protection and find out her greatest secret of all?

CHAPTER 10

After Abby left for the evening, Winnie puttered around the shop, putting things away and straightening and rearranging things on the shelves. She had put an apron with the store's logo of a cute baby wolf with a tree and moon in the background over her t-shirt and jeans and pulled out a feather duster. She was enjoying the fantasy that this was her shop. One day she hoped to open something similar: maybe in Rivelou, maybe somewhere else. She hadn't decided yet.

The shop of her dreams was called "Winnie's Witchy Whimsies." It would carry a cross between the merchandise that Abby had here with some of the more arcane items that Salvia's store displayed.

Winnie was so busy building her shop in the sky that she didn't notice the bells on the door ring until a voice called out, "Hey, can someone help me?"

The customer, a woman Winnie recognized as a regular patron, wanted some of the fancy cheeses, dips, and crackers put together on a charcuterie board for a spur-of-the-moment party she was throwing.

Winnie prepared everything, rang up a nice sum at the cash register, and by the time she was done, had several customers waiting in line.

"Abby is going to be glad she took the night off," Winnie thought, looking at the customer-packed store. She was so busy for the next hour that she had no more time to daydream about having her own store. In fact, she began to wonder if being a shopkeeper was such a good idea.

Maybe she could be a researcher. She'd taken Dr. Fontaine's Anthropology 101 course last year and had enjoyed it a lot. She could become the female Dr. Fontaine and write books and do speaking engagements. "Dr. Winifred Thorne." It had a nice ring to it.

She wondered idly where the man had gone. She'd been

looking forward to taking another class with him this spring—the fact that he'd been quite handsome despite being ancient—at least 40 she was sure—hadn't hurt her interest in taking another of his classes. But Fontaine had left the university suddenly, and no one seemed to know what had happened to him.

Hm, maybe she could practice her magic and try to scry for him. Wouldn't it make her the talk of the university if she could definitely find out where the professor had gone?

Her musings were interrupted when the door chimed again, and another new customer appeared. This time she knew him quite well.

"Hey Tyler," she said, as he started to browse, trying hard not to look at her. He seemed a bit embarrassed to be in the store, she noted with a silent laugh. "You looking for something special? This isn't usually your type of place."

Tyer was a good guy. She'd known him since high school. She was aware that he was a shapeshifter, a wolf in fact. Sometimes the wolves and witches and the other paranormals in her high school had banded into cliques. But Tyler was one of those people who seemed to get along with everyone.

"Yeah," he said, shuffling his feet and looking at the floor. "I need to get a gift for my oldest sister, Ana. There's an engagement party for her in about a week. I saw you through the window, and I thought, 'Winnie's a girl; maybe she'd know something my sister would like.'"

"So glad you noticed I'm a girl," Winnie said sarcastically.

"Come on, Winnie. You know I didn't mean it like that."

Winnie took pity on him. "Yeah," she said, bumping his shoulder. "I know what you mean. And I should be able to help you. Ana comes in here a lot, so I have a good idea of some stuff that she likes."

She brought him over to a display of afghans in the school colors of red, black, and silver. "I know she's always admiring these afghans, but I'm not sure you want to splurge that much; they are kind of expensive."

"Yeah," he grimaced, looking at the price tag. "Maybe I can get my brother Dan to go in with me. That would make it more affordable."

"Hey, good idea. Why don't you talk to him about it? You have several days to make up your mind."

"That's true. I'll talk to Dan. And have you heard the rumors?"

"What rumors?"

"About the latest Artificial Witch murder?"

"I heard there had been another girl murdered today. Do they think it is related to the other two? I can't figure out who would be doing something like this. My cousin Dave won't tell me anything," Winnie pouted. "He's a cop, you know. But he thinks I'm just a kid."

"Luckily, Chris, he's my future brother-in-law, the guy who's gonna marry Ana, talks to the police chief a lot."

"Yeah, I've heard about him. He's a Hunter, right?"

"Yeah, that's the one. But he's a good guy, even so. I really like him, and he's good for Ana and Sophie—she's actually my niece, but she's not that much younger than me. And my grandpa likes him—and that really counts for a lot. He hated Ana's first husband, and he was only a non-para."

"So, what did Chris tell you?" Winnie asked, hoping to get her friend back on track. She'd had a lot of experience over the years with Tyler's round-about method of communication.

"Oh yeah. He said they think they know who the victim is, but they haven't made it public yet because her parents haven't been identified. But it was definitely someone who went to high school with us."

Winnie put her hand to her mouth. "Oh Goddess, Tyler, no! I can't believe that! Do you think it was anyone we know?"

"Well, yeah. The school wasn't that big, and it's someone who is here at U of R with us now." He used the initials for the University of Rivelou.

"Hey, Winnie, are you okay?" He came and put his arm around her. "I didn't mean to upset you. Maybe they're wrong."

"No, I'm sure they aren't wrong. And I have a terrible feeling I know who it is, Tyler."

"How can you know that?"

"Ashley. You remember Ashley Butler, right?"

"Yeah, of course I do. She was right behind me all the way from kindergarten on whenever we lined up alphabetically. You know, Bertrand, Butler. She was next in the alphabet. She's a really nice girl. But why would it be her?"

"She wasn't in class this morning. She's in my English 101 class. She's always there. She's a really good student. She'd never miss a class unless..."

Tyler finished the thought for her. "Unless she's dead."

CHAPTER 11

Shannon avoided listening to any news over the weekend. She had a great excuse. She spent most of Saturday and again Sunday morning working with Ana on painting the guest bedroom. Since Sophie was with them on Saturday, they made sure to keep the talk to Ana's and Chris's upcoming wedding.

Sophie made it easy; she was thrilled with the fact that her mother was marrying Chris. It was obvious she already loved him. "And who wouldn't," Shannon thought with all the affection and pride of a sister. Her brother was a wonderful guy.

Sophie had opinions on everything from the color of the flowers and what style of dress she should wear as a junior bridesmaid to how they should incorporate the usual shifter vows to include Chris, who after all was both a Hunter and a witch. "Even if his powers aren't that strong," she told Shannon in no uncertain terms when Shannon objected to using the term "witch" for her brother.

"Well, he really doesn't think of himself that way," she explained to Sophie. "He thinks of himself as a Hunter, the person who polices the evil in the paranormal world, not as a witch."

"Well, he couldn't do that if he didn't have some power, now could he?" Sophie asked in her, "I'm going to explain it slowly and carefully to the clueless adult," voice. "Mom, what did you and Dad do at your wedding?" she asked, effectively ending the discussion.

"Well, you know we eloped, Honey, and your dad didn't know anything about shifters. Grandpa was just as happy to use the elopement as an excuse not to do any of the regular rituals and keep your dad in the dark."

"Well, if you had just told him, it might have been easier for him," Sophie said in defense of her father.

"I'm sure your mom and the rest of the pack had good reasons," Shannon began. She could sense the tension building between the mother and daughter.

Ana dispelled it with a laugh. "I'd have had to have bitten your dad and 'made' him. Can you really see how he would have reacted to becoming a werewolf?"

Sophie laughed, too. "Yeah, that wouldn't have gone over so well, would it? And besides, then I wouldn't have a new baby brother."

Sophie was already in love with one-day-old Jonathan Jr. even though she wouldn't meet him until the next day.

"Of course Jonathan has named the baby after himself. He's hoping for a little 'mini-me,' I guess," said Shannon, not disguising her opinion of the arrogant Jonathan Dugan. "I hope Melanie is strong enough to exert her influence on the child so he's not too insufferable." She had forgotten that Ana tried to keep criticism of Jonathan to a minimum in front of Sophie.

"Maybe we can find an infant-sized business suit for him," Ana said, deflecting the comment. Sophie ran with the idea, immediately getting on her phone to check out cute infant outfits for the baby.

Shannon was just glad she hadn't inadvertently caused a problem between mother and daughter.

The rest of the day passed without any friction, and Shannon and Ana finished the painting project on Sunday morning without Sophie, who was finally meeting her new baby brother.

The room looked great. It had been a relaxing way to take her mind off Friday's events, but as late Sunday afternoon rolled around, and she and Dave were starting in on their two weeks of night duty, she had to get back to reality.

Thank goodness the temperatures had headed back down to normal for a western Kentucky spring. The overnight low was expected to be a comfortable 57 degrees. Shannon walked into the locker room and was stopped short by the sight of the usual cheerful Dave. He hadn't finished putting on his uniform. His shirt lay on the bench beside him; his chest was bare. He was sitting with his head in his hands, shoulders hunched. Something was wrong.

"Hey, what is it?" she asked, heading over to her own

locker to put her things away and change.

"You didn't hear? They finally announced the name of the girl who was murdered Friday."

"No, I have to admit I've avoided the news as much as possible. Who was it? Did you know her?"

"Her name was Ashley Butler. She was just 19. I didn't really know her; not enough that I recognized her when I saw the body. But she was a friend of my cousin Winnie's. I remembered her name when I heard it. I hadn't seen her since she was a kid. They used to play together all the time when they were little. She graduated with Winnie from Chandler County High School. I think they'd grown apart the last few years, but still. This is going to hit Winnie hard."

He looked up, and Shannon saw the sorrow in his dark brown eyes. She wanted to take the pain away. To soothe him. She started to put a hand on his still-bare shoulder, then stopped the gesture before Dave noticed. "You think of Winnie like a little sister, don't you?" She sat down next to him so they could talk. She told herself that she did not feel the heat of his thigh as Dave shifted and bumped against her. No. She did not, and she didn't enjoy it, either, she told herself. She was just comforting her partner.

"Yeah, I don't have any sisters or brothers, neither does she. So even though there's over ten years' difference in our ages, we've always been close. I'm really protective of her. Used to babysit her when she was little. I guess part of me still sees her as that little girl running around with her 'Minerva the Witch' doll."

Shannon smiled. "Yeah, I had one of those too. Maybe we can stop by The Wolf's Den while we're on patrol. If Winnie's working there tonight, you can talk to her. See how she's doing."

"Good idea, thanks." He turned to his locker and put on his uniform shirt. "At least it isn't as hot tonight," he said, obviously trying to change the subject. "It's a lot more comfortable to wear all this gear on a cool night."

"If this is really a paranormal murder, what good will all of this," she pointed to herself, "the taser, the Kevlar vest, the pepper spray, do they do anything against something paranormal?"

"Well, I can tell you from personal experience a witch is affected by pepper spray. Make sure you hit them with it the first time, or they may be able to turn it around on you. As for the rest, that's why you need me to start training you. You just never know what you're going to run into in Rivelou."

Shannon made a noncommittal remark as they headed to their patrol car. She really didn't want to think about taking up witchcraft again.

Their usual route took them past the university and the strip of stores across from it, so The Wolf's Den was their first stop. They found Winnie behind the counter, sniffling and trying to look as if she were okay.

"Hey, Kid, I know Abby will let you go home early if it's too much for you here," Dave said, giving his cousin a fierce hug.

"I've told her she can go home," said Abby, who was also behind the counter. "But she says she wants to stay. We're only open a couple of more hours anyway."

"She's right; I want to be here. It's easier if I have something to do. Mom and Dad are acting like they want to wrap me up in bubble wrap, add a couple of protection spells, and never let me leave the house again."

"I understand that. I know it bothers you, but I do understand how they feel; I feel the same. There are three girls your age who are dead. We all just want to protect you."

"They weren't witches—I am. They didn't have the same ability to protect themselves as I do," Winnie said.

Shannon had been standing near the door; she had only met Winnie the one time and figured it was better for David and Abby to do the talking. Now she couldn't help but step in. "Just because you have power doesn't mean you're always protected against evil."

"Oh, what do you know? You don't even use the power you do have."

"Hey, Winnie, that's not like you," said Dave.

"Well you've said it yourself—you think Shannon should use her powers. And that's what got Ashley killed. She's always wanted power—was jealous of my power. That's why we stopped being friends in high school. She couldn't stand that I had something she didn't."

"Winnie, how did Ashley know you were a witch?" Abby asked slowly. "You know the code. You don't tell anyone. Ever."

"I didn't tell her. It wasn't me. I'm not sure who it was," Winnie said defensively, not meeting anyone's eyes. "Maybe it was Willow or Kenzy."

"And you think maybe Ashley got in with someone who promised to teach her witchcraft? Give her power?" Abby asked.

"I don't know. It could be." Winnie looked down and played with the hem of her T-shirt. Shannon wondered if Dave was picking up on the signs that the girl knew something she wasn't telling. Or was he too close to her to see it? "What about the other girls who died, Winnie?" she asked. "Did they want to be witches, too? Did they hang out with Ashley?"

"I didn't know them. They both went to the university, but they weren't from around here. I never met them."

This time, Winnie looked Shannon straight in the eyes. "I just know that if someone promised to teach Ashley witchcraft, she would have fallen for it."

"I'm glad you told us this, Kiddo." Dave squeezed her shoulders. "It might be the information we need to help us. You know I'm going to do everything I can to find out who did this, and so are Shannon and the rest of the department."

CHAPTER 12

"Winnie knows more than she's saying," Shannon said. They were back in their patrol car. It had been a quiet night so far. They had patrolled the downtown area, along the river, and had headed out to make sure nothing was going on at the Mounds near where the murder had occurred. The biggest event of the night had been sending home a few drunks who were partying too noisily outside one of the bars.

"Why would you say that?" Dave asked sharply.

"It's the way she reacted when she talked about Ashley wanting to be a witch. She couldn't look you in the eye."

"Winnie's a good kid. She wouldn't do anything wrong."

"I didn't say she'd done anything terrible, just that she knows more than she told you. You've never done anything you felt ashamed of? Never did anything stupid when you were a teen? David Thorne the Perfect, patron saint of witches?"

"God, Shannon. What is it you have against me? First I'm too young and green to know anything. Now I act like a saint. And apparently whatever you think about me is spilling over onto how you see Winnie."

"That is so unfair. Maybe you're too close to Winnie. You didn't notice how she was acting."

"Maybe you're just prejudiced because she admits she's a witch, and she's related to me."

Shannon pulled off the road near Mitchell Park, a small square in the neighborhood near her home on Westbridge Street. It just happened to be the area where Alexander Fontaine had killed an unsuspecting jogger one night last fall.

"How about you are the most insufferable man I've known since... since..." She stopped. Why had she been about to say he was just like Jason, her husband? Dave was nothing like Jason.

"Since who?"

She was silent. Dave proved her thought about being

clueless by totally not noticing that she was suddenly upset.

After waiting a moment for her to answer, he asked again, more gently this time. "Since who, Shannon? What were you going to say?"

"Since no one. No one has ever been as insufferable as you are." She started to put the motor into gear again when he stopped her with a hand on the wheel.

"You were about to say since Jason, weren't you? It's okay, you know. From everything I've heard from you, he was a good guy. I'd be proud if you thought I were like him."

Shannon huffed a long breath. Damn it, he wasn't as clueless as she'd thought. And didn't that just piss her off even more. She needed to stay angry right now, or she was going to cry. And that just wouldn't do. Dave would never let her hear the end of it... or he'd comfort her. And that would be even worse.

"No, you are nothing like Jason. He was kind, and thoughtful, and... and..." Dammit. Here came the tears.

Dave drew her gently across the bench seat of the cruiser and held her, patting her on the back in the same way he had done for his cousin. "It's okay, Shannon. I'm sorry. I can't imagine how terrible it was to lose him in that way."

He lifted her chin and tenderly ran his thumbs across her cheeks to dry the tears. His hand moved up and down her back. It began slowly, like you'd comfort a child, then became more sensual. She felt mesmerized as she stared into his dark eyes. He leaned in ever so slowly, the way you'd approach a frightened kitten. As if he expected her to run or hiss. But she didn't want to run.

It was slow and sweet. His lips barely touched hers. When she didn't pull away, he pulled her closer, deepening the kiss. His tongue asked for permission, and she parted her lips. Their tongues played with each other in a gentle dance. Yes. This was what she had wanted. It had been so long. No one had touched her in this way since Jason. And at the thought of her husband, she suddenly pushed away.

"What the hell, Dave! Why would you do that?"

She straightened her uniform shirt and quickly put the car in Drive, pulling out of the parking spot with a squeal of tires as if they'd just gotten an emergency call.

"Hey, I'm sorry. You were crying and I just…"

"You just what? Wanted to get some?"

"No! That's not what I meant. I was trying to comfort you."

"By sticking your tongue in my mouth? Some way to comfort a person."

"You weren't objecting, you know. I would have pulled back… I did pull back as soon as you did."

"That's not the point. You know how I feel. I'm a widow. And I'm too old for you."

"My God, Shannon, you wrap your dead husband around you like a shield. Are you not allowed to ever have feelings for anyone again just because he died? And I'm only three years younger than you, anyway."

He mentally rolled his eyes at himself. Yeah, that last part had sounded real mature. Kind of like a kid in grade school.

"Look, let's just forget it ever happened," Shannon said.

"Sure, if that's what you want."

But Shannon didn't think she was going to forget how soft his lips has been as he kissed her, how strong his arms had felt around her. How safe and secure she had felt when he held her.

They rode in awkward silence for several blocks.

"Well," Dave thought, "might as well go all the way. She's already upset with me." He grinned to himself as he realized the innuendo.

"On Friday you said you'd think about letting me coach you in some magic, maybe help you open up some of those channels so at least you'll know when you're around another paranormal."

Shannon turned and looked at him for a moment, then put her eyes back on the road.

"Are you out of your mind? First you…" She paused, and he could see she didn't even want to say the word kiss in connection with him.

While silently shouting, "Yes!" because he could tell she had enjoyed that kiss as much as he had, he tried to think of a better reason for her to allow him to coach her. "I'm only thinking of your career, you know. It's only going to help you if the other paranormals on the force know you aren't hiding anything."

"You mean like murdering three girls?" she asked sarcastically.

"Dammit! Why do you have to take everything I say the wrong way?"

"Well, why do you have to be such a stubborn ass?"

"I'm not being…"

"What about getting all huffy when I just suggested Winnie might be feeling guilty about the murders?"

"She's not feeling guilty. She's got nothing to feel guilty about. It's different."

"Oh, how so?

"It just is."

Shannon took a deep breath. This was getting them no place. She couldn't keep arguing with her partner. It was distracting, and there were too many things that could happen while on patrol to let a squabble interfere with their work. "Look, how about a bargain?"

"What kind of bargain?" David asked suspiciously.

"I'll let you give me a few basic magic lessons if you'll talk to Winnie again and see what it is that has her so weirded out."

"She's not…"

With a smug smile she turned to him for a moment before looking back at the road. "That's easier for me then. You don't talk to Winnie—and let me be with you when you do—and I don't have to do any magic lessons."

David ground his teeth. "Alright. You win. Lessons in witchcraft for you, and we'll both talk to Winnie."

CHAPTER 13

"No time like the present," Dave said. They had changed back into civilian clothes and stowed all of their equipment in their lockers.

"What?" Shannon asked, pretending not to know what he meant.

"No time like the present to start your lessons. In fact, it's almost midnight. The perfect hour."

Shannon fidgeted with her purse, trying to look as if she were searching for something inside. It didn't work.

"Shannon. You know it's true. You need to do this." Dave tried to put all of his persuasive powers into his voice. "Wish I was the captain," he thought. "I'd just use my siren powers to make her do what's best for her." But he knew he would never try to coerce her in that way or in any other way. If Shannon were going to accept him and accept who she was—both the good and the bad—she was going to have to do it on her own. And if he did use witchcraft to persuade her about her own magic, she'd never believe he hadn't used it to coerce her into a relationship with him.

And that's what he wanted. If he hadn't been sure before he kissed her, he was now. There had been a spark between them. As soon as he touched her lips he felt it, and even if she weren't ready to acknowledge it, he knew she had also.

He watched her take a deep breath.

"Okay. Your place or mine?"

At that moment a couple of other officers walked into the locker room. And to make it worse, they were detectives, not just patrol officers.

Shannon turned bright red. "Oh God, that's not what I meant! I know what you must have thought but it didn't come out right. We weren't... we aren't..."

Dave suppressed an urge to chuckle at Shannon's embarrassment. That wouldn't make any points with her. And luckily, the detectives were Tony Abello and Jake Waseaux. Jake was a witch, and Tony was a bobcat shifter.

"Hey guys, Shannon has agreed to let me help her with her magic," he said quickly. "We were just talking about the best place to practice."

"That's excellent, Shannon. I'll look forward to seeing you at the next coven meeting. Merry meet." Jake used the traditional greeting.

"And merry part," Shannon replied. "I look forward to it." Her mother might have practiced on the dark side of the craft, but she'd taught her children to be polite, Shannon told herself as she hurried out of the locker room. And damn her fair complexion. She knew she was still as bright red as a tomato.

"Hey, wait up," Dave called, catching her by the back door.

"I have never been so embarrassed in my life."

"Don't worry. They don't think we're up to anything. They're just happy you're coming out of the closet. Another active paranormal on the force will make their lives easier—someone they can call on if the crime involves something that isn't nonpara."

They walked out to the parking lot. "Look, why don't you follow me back to my place. I've got all the supplies we need already there."

"Okay, that makes sense."

He gave her his address. He lived on the west side of town in a small, two-bedroom bungalow out in the country. There were no neighbors in sight, she noticed when she arrived.

"This is nice," she said as she got out of her car and walked over to Dave as he dismounted his Harley.

"Yeah, I inherited it from my grandparents. It's small, but it's all I need, and it's secluded so no one will complain if I host a wild orgy." He laughed at the look she gave him as he guided her up the steps.

"Wild beer parties with your motorcycle buddies is more how I see it," she said.

"You just wait until Midsummer's Night," he said playfully. He stopped suddenly just inside the door. "Oh God, I just realized. No, that's not true' I already knew it, but it just hit me again now that I know one of the girls who was killed. That's when the next murder will be."

He ran his hands through his hair in the gesture he always used when frustrated. "We've got to get this figured out, Shannon, before someone else is killed."

"I know. I don't want any more young girls dying because they want to become witches when they're not."

"You really think that's what this is all about? I don't know what's worse, some random psycho who kills girls like we've been telling the public or someone who's sacrificing them in some artificial game because they're a wannabe witch."

"But you know that's what everyone on the force—at least everyone with power thinks. Now that it's hit close to home you just want to ignore the facts. And you're afraid that Winnie is in danger," Shannon said.

He winced; she was the one who'd just hit too close to the truth. "You know, I really hate it when you're right."

Shannon smirked. "See, that's what I've been trying to tell you. Listen to me, Kid, and you'll learn something. But seriously, did either of the first two victims have power? We know that Ashley didn't. Were the others into witchcraft at all? Has anyone looked at it from that angle? Remember, no one's told me much of anything about the murders except you," Shannon said a little bitterly. "Am I still a suspect, by the way?"

I'm sure Chief Anderson doesn't think you are any longer, and I know his opinion will go a long way with the rest of the force, particularly the paranormals. Didn't you notice how Tony and Jake reacted to you tonight when you told them you were going to take lessons from me? I bet they tell everyone else you're okay, too. You'll see."

"You're sure? This being a murder suspect has been really getting to me. And if I'm allowed to look at the evidence, I do think maybe I can help everyone see it from this new angle. I have an idea of where to start."

"Really? Where? Damn it, you're sidetracking me again. You really do need to work on your spells before we do anything else." Dave turned and motioned for her to follow him down the hall. "Let's go to my workroom. We can talk about this later after we finish your first lesson. Do you remember how to create a protection circle?"

"A protection circle?" Shannon questioned.

"You know, to keep dark forces, spirits, demons, anything evil or unwanted out when you're performing a ritual."

"Uh… my mother never tried to keep those things away. In fact, she actively called to them. So no, I don't know anything about protection circles."

"Huh. Right. I guess I'm starting to better understand some of your problems with the craft. We're starting with the basics, then."

CHAPTER 14

He opened the door onto his workroom, which was in the smaller of the two bedrooms in his home. It was simply furnished with an old oak chest of drawers on one wall where he kept his supplies. Heavy curtains of navy velvet hung at the two windows to both keep the light out and to make sure no one could see in. The center of the room was bare except for a small table in the middle.

Dave went to the chest of drawers and began pulling things out, mumbling to himself as he did so.

He handed her a piece of chalk. "Draw a circle on the floor around the table. Make sure it's big enough for both of us to stand inside."

As she knelt down and drew a wide circle on the oak floorboards, he stripped off his shirt. "Don't worry, that's all I'm taking off," he said with a smirk when she looked up at him. She quickly looked back down at the line she was drawing. She didn't want him to notice her admiring his very nice abs.

He stepped over the line she had drawn and placed several candles of different colors, two crystals, a bell, a book, and bowls of salt and water on the table in the center. "Step inside, then watch what I do."

She stood up but hesitated outside the circle.

He smiled at her. "Don't worry. It's perfectly safe. This is white magic, not dark. Once I've set the circle nothing can come in and hurt you."

He held out his hand. She hesitated for a moment, then grasped it and stepped over the chalk line. She felt a connection, a spark, when she took his hand. Was it his power calling to her? Or something more elemental?

Dave kept her hand; his dark eyes seemed to see right through her as he looked at her intently. "You feel it too, don't you? It's something we're definitely going to have to explore later."

She looked away, confused by her conflicting emotions.

He let go of her hand and turned to the table. Taking the bowl of salt, he sprinkled it over the chalk line she had drawn, making sure there were no gaps and her line was evenly covered. Softly he chanted, his voice soothing to her.

"By earth's pure essence, this circle I make,
No harm may enter or dark power take
Earth, Water, Fire, Air
Here my prayer
for protection.
In this ring I stand apart
From all ill-will that darkens my heart.
As I will, so mote it be."

He stopped for a moment. "This spell helps to cleanse our hearts and our souls of any evil intent and wards us from any negative energies or spirits that might be lurking. It's an important part of working as a white witch. I'll ask you to memorize it later."

Shannon nodded, reassured by the words he had recited. This was vastly different from the way her mother had begun ceremonies, usually with blood from an animal, or maybe even a human.

Next he placed a candle at each of the cardinal points. "Yellow for earth," he explained as he put it at the north. He crossed over and placed the red candle opposite it. "Red for fire at the southern point. Blue for air." He put that candle on the east side of the circle. "And green for water." He put the final one in the west.

"Now we ask the spirits to guide me in teaching you."

He walked around the circle lighting the candles and invoking the creatures and spirits at each cardinal point.

Shannon just nodded and watched him closely as he recited,

"By the crone and the maiden,
I call upon the spirits of knowledge to awaken
This student eager to learn the craft,
Potions and spells for good to cast.
May love and understanding replace her fears.

Joy and happiness chase away her tears.
Earth, Air, Fire, and Water
Shower your blessings on your daughter.
As I will so mote it be."

As he finished the chant his chest and arms began to glow, and she could see that he was covered with swirling tattoos. The light that emanated from them, from him, was beautiful, multi-colored, ethereal.

He took a deep breath and turned to her. "Let's see what you remember. You said you had called fire before?"

"Yes, but air is my natural element. I was better with that."

"Still, let's start with fire. Believe it or not, it's less dangerous to a beginner than air—we don't want you creating a tornado in the house."

"I'd be excited if I could just call enough air to blow out one of those candles, but I do see your point," she laughed.

David was glad to see she was relaxed enough to be amused. He loved her laugh though he rarely heard it. The fact that she felt at ease now was a good sign.

They spent the next few hours going through the spell to make fire. She was hot and sweaty, not to mention exhausted, when finally she got it right.

"Look, look I did it, Dave!" she said excitedly, showing her hand where a small flame flickered.

"You sure did, my little witch," he said.

"I am not little!"

"Not in power, no. You have all you need," he said.

She jumped at him and gave him a kiss. And before she realized what he was doing, he had doused the flames—both the candles and the one in her hand—with a flick of his fingers, and they were kissing passionately.

He picked her up and headed into the hallway and to his bedroom.

CHAPTER 15

The air between them crackled, charged with a force that was different from the magic Shannon had felt when calling fire a few moments before. She hadn't felt like this since Jason. She shook her head. She wasn't going to think about her husband right now. David had been right; Jason would never have wanted her to spend the rest of her life mourning him. She owed it to his memory to go on living. And she hadn't felt this alive in a long, long time.

Her fingers grazed Dave's arm where his tattoos were still glowing golden in the dark bedroom. The touch sent a shimmer of warmth through her. He carefully laid her back on his bed and just stood staring at her.

"By the goddess, Shannon, you are beautiful. You don't know how long I've wanted you like this. Here… in my bed."

His words made her feel powerful. Jason had been her first, and so far only, lover. They'd come together as inexperienced virgins, fumbling and floundering from first kiss to more. They had understood that neither one had more experience than the other. There had been a comfort in that. Neither one had ever felt awkward or worried that they might say or do something embarrassingly naïve.

But Shannon knew that David was much more sophisticated than she was in this area. Oh, she might lord the three years' difference in their age over him while they were on patrol, but it was really because she felt insecure and inexperienced around him. Now, hearing him tell her that he had wanted her—fantasized about her—gave her a courage she had never known she had.

And the one thing she and Jason had never been able to share was her power, her magic. Jason was a non-para after all, and she'd stomped down that part of herself fiercely when they made love, even before she had rejected magic altogether.

Now, as she opened her powers to David, she could feel

the pulse of his magic along with hers. It was like a steady beat beneath her fingertips, responding to her own power. He flicked a hand toward the candles that sat on his dresser, lighting them. The ones in this room were all pink or red for passion and desire.

In the glow of the candlelight she watched as his brown eyes darkened even more, reflecting her own passion.

"I can feel your magic," she whispered, voice thick with desire. "It's in the air… between us."

David tilted his head to the side, the corners of his lips curving into a mischievous smile. "It's more than that, Shannon. You feel me, and I feel you. Every beat of your heart, every surge of your power. It's like a spell we've been casting since the moment we met."

Without breaking eye contact, his hand found her waist, pulling her against him. She could feel the heat even through her clothing.

"You're like a lovely birthday present just waiting for me to unwrap. You know there is a magical way I could do that, don't you?"

Shannon nodded slowly, her eyes never leaving his.

"But right now I want to unwrap this package slowly, to savor every moment." He reached for her blouse and began to unbutton the top button. He took his time, savoring, just as he had said. He bent down and kissed her neck, then her chest, then opened a few more buttons and spread the blouse, exposing the white sports bra she had worn to work.

She rolled her eyes in embarrassment as he ran his fingers over the practical cotton. He noticed her blush.

"Don't worry. I know you didn't dress to entice me when you got ready for work. I think that makes it all the sexier that you're here with me now."

He bent down and kissed her nipple through her bra. Shannon squirmed and made a breathless little mewling sound.

"You like that?" David asked, sitting back up and looking at her.

"Yes."

"Then let's try a little more. He pulled the shirt and bra over her head and gazed with appreciation at her pale skin and pink nipples.

"God, you're beautiful, Shannon."

She moved to place her hands over her breasts, embarrassed. "No one but…"

"No one but Jason has ever seen you this way? Don't worry; I won't be offended if you say his name. He was your husband, your first love. I understand you might think of him when we make love."

"Well maybe if you let me…" She reached up and ran her hands over his chest. She caught her breath as she looked at him. During their lesson she hadn't had the time to look closely at his tattoos. "I don't understand," she said as she traced an elaborate design with a pentagram at the center, surrounded by the moon, stars, and planets. A dragon played in the center of this universe. "I don't understand your tattoos. Why did I never see them before? And why do they glow now?"

"They enhance my magic. They only appear when I've been practicing witchcraft or when I'm feeling particularly impassioned about something—or someone."

"And you feel impassioned about me?"

"You haven't been able to tell?"

"I guess I've been too caught up in my own head to have noticed much of anything around me. But I'm glad you dragged me out of that place and back into the real world." She smiled and again ran her hands over the hard planes of muscle on his chest and arms. He felt so good. "Mmm," she murmured.

"Shannon, you're killing me here." Her touch seemed to ignite the space between them, the heat of their bodies mingled, and a powerful energy swirled around them. His tattoos glowed ever brighter as he bent to kiss her again, and she felt their powers merge. Their magic was not two separate things; instead, his power and hers danced together, intertwining into something new, something greater. The longer he kissed her, the more they joined until she could no longer tell where he left off and she began.

They drew away for a moment, his hands still on her waist, hers around his neck. But she didn't want even this much distance between them. Her lips brushed his again as they had earlier, tentative at first, but the electric pull between them deepened the kiss. His breath hitched, and Shannon's own magic surged. A wave of heat radiated from her core. Her hand continued to slide up and down his chest and came to rest over his heart. "It's so good to feel you." She loved feeling the warmth of his skin. He was vibrant and alive. She traced her fingers along his collarbone, reveling in the shiver that ran through him.

David's hands imitated hers, exploring her back, her shoulders, her breasts. He bent lower and kissed her breast again, his dark beard prickly against the soft skin, making her writhe and whimper. He reached tentatively for the button of her jeans. "May I?" he asked softly. "I'll understand if this is all you're ready for."

Even as he said it his traitorous cock jumped as she reached down and touched him through his own jeans. She let out a soft moan. "I want more, David. I think I'm ready for so much more."

Ever so slowly he pulled down her zipper, his fingers exploring lower and lower, tantalizing her. Finally he reached beneath her panties and caressed the curls between her legs.

"Oh God," she said as she squirmed against his hand. His touch was gentle, yet she could tell he wanted more, too. She moaned again. "Too many clothes," she said, pushing at his jeans. "Get rid of these now."

"Your wish is my command." He gave her a mischievous grin again, flicked his hand, and in a blink he was kneeling naked over her. His magic swirled in the air; she could see it shimmering in the candlelight, then slowly fading away.

"Shannon," he murmured, his voice low, his breath hot against her skin as he leaned over her. "You have no idea what you do to me."

She grinned back and reached between them, running her hands up and down his hard length. "I think I do."

He whispered another incantation, and the air was filled with the scent of lavender and roses, the flowers of a summer garden, although it was still spring and nothing was blooming yet.

He groaned softly, moving his head lower, kissing her

core. His touch was sure as he worshiped the most sensitive part of her body, his beard once again adding another layer of sensation. Her breath caught, and her body responded, her magic surging again in answer to his touch. He nipped and sucked as she squirmed, and his fingers entered her even as he continued to drive her out of her mind with his tongue.

"That's it; let go. Let me make you feel good," he said, his mouth still against her core. He sucked her once again, and she could stand it no longer. Her hips bucked; she moaned his name as her world seemed to explode around her.

She was breathing heavily. It had never been like this with Jason. Maybe it was the power she and David shared, but she didn't really care what the reason was right now. His lips moved slowly back up her body, and their lips met once again, even more urgently this time, tongues tangling and dancing. She pressed herself against him, moaning and writhing.

"Shannon," he whispered. "I want to feel every part of you."

She murmured her surrender as he parted her legs and entered her. Slowly, slowly, the desire built between them, their bodies moving together as one.

Every touch sent sparks of magic through Shannon. Yes, this was different, this was new. She knew, now that she had opened herself to Dave, opened herself to this sharing of his magic and hers, she could never go back. She had cut off a piece of herself by denying her power. Dave had come along and put her back together again. Even as she thought it, the sensations ramped up again, and they shattered together, calling each other's names.

CHAPTER 16

The sun was high in the sky when Shannon opened her eyes. She blinked. Where was she? The white curtains that blew in the soft, early morning breeze from the open window weren't hers. She sat up quickly as her memory returned. Dave... candles... fire flickering in her hand... And after. Oh Lord, what had she done?

Beside her the man in question stirred and reached out sleepily for her. "Lie back down, little witch, and let's see if we can do it all again."

"Oh no. No, no, no. I made a mistake. I'm so sorry, Dave." Shannon jumped from the bed and scrambled around the floor in search of her clothes.

"Shannon, what's wrong?" Dave sat up in bed and ran his hands through his hair, trying to catch up with Shannon's mercurial mood change. The night had been magical... and now this?

"I shouldn't have let anything happen. I know what I said last night, but I was wrong. It's my fault, not yours. I'm sorry," she said as she pulled on her jeans and searched the covers for her bra.

"This is about Jason, isn't it?" Dave asked, getting out of bed and reaching for her.

"Yes, of course it's about Jason. What else would it be about?"

"Last night I thought you were ready to..."

"Last night I was caught up in the moment, in the magic, in sharing our power. I should never have betrayed my husband."

"Shannon, your husband is dead. You are not betraying him. You said yourself he would have wanted you to move on, to find someone else." His voice was too loud, too forceful. He knew it, but he couldn't seem to stop himself or tamp down his frustration.

"Well, I was wrong, alright? It's wrong, what we did. I'm

not ready to find someone else. Damn it, where is my purse?" She headed to the living room, found her purse, and headed out the door as quickly as possible. Dave quickly pulled on his pants and followed her to the porch. He stared after her as she made it to her car, opened the door, and gunned the motor as she took off down his gravel driveway as fast as she could.

"Oh God," she thought as she sped away. She was going to have to work next to Dave all night—every night. There was no way she could ask for a new partner. Not right now. She'd barely got out from under suspicion of murder. Asking for a new partner because she had slept with her current one wasn't going to cut it. *Suck it up, buttercup. You're just going to have to be cool, calm, and professional. At all times. No more teasing or kidding around with Dave. And no more witchcraft lessons.* That's what had gotten her into trouble. It always got her into trouble. The damn witchcraft.

As she began to calm down, her empty belly made itself known. She looked at the clock on her dashboard. It had been close to dawn when they went to bed. Now it was after 1 p.m. She hadn't eaten anything since last night's dinner, and she had to be back at work at 5 p.m. She punched a few numbers on her dashboard and called Abby on her cell. "Hey girl, can you do a late lunch?"

"For you? Of course. But what's up?"

"Nothing. Nothing's up. I just need to grab lunch before I go back on duty. I'll see you in about twenty minutes." Shannon hung up quickly. She knew she would end up telling Abby everything, but she really didn't want to do it over the phone, especially not while driving.

A short time later she pulled up at The Wolf's Den.

"Hey Shannon, I'll tell Abby you're here," Winnie said when she walked in the door.

"Yeah, thanks." She had said she wanted to talk more to Winnie about her friend and the other murdered girls. She'd promised David they'd do it together. Now was not the time for it, though. She was still too upset about what had happened with Dave to pull off any kind of interrogation.

She pretended to look at the merchandise when Winnie

came back into the sales area. She really could not make small talk with Dave's cousin right now. She felt as if "I slept with David Thorne" were tattooed across her forehead. Tattoos. Damn. Why did she have to think about tattoos right now? About Dave's sexy, magical tattoos. About his soft beard and dark brown eyes. His slow, sexy kisses... She shook her head, trying to get the picture of Dave standing naked before her, tattoos glowing in the candlelight, out of her mind.

When Abby came out front, they quickly decided on a little diner in the next block. "I've got to get home and shower and change before I go into work," she explained when Abby first suggested a relaxing meal at a well-known lunch spot on the river.

When they got to the diner it was late enough that they had their choice of booths and picked one in the back for privacy.

"Ok, tell me what this is all about," Abby said as soon as the waitress had taken their orders.

"I can't just want to have lunch with my best friend?"

"Sure you can, but that's not what this is. I could hear it in your voice when you called. You're upset about something, so spill."

"I had sex with David."

"Ooo, you go, girl! How was it? Is he as good in bed as his reputation?"

"He has a reputation?" The jealousy that welled up in her at the thought of Dave with other women—enough women to have a "reputation"—startled her. She had nothing to be jealous about. Nothing at all. "Oh, forget I said that. Of course he does; everyone says he's a player. And I don't care how great the sex was; it's not going to happen again."

"Shannon, Honey, what is it? What's wrong? Did David do something to upset you?"

"I betrayed Jason; I betrayed my husband. I should never have been attracted to Dave in the first place, and then he suckered me in with a lesson in witchcraft. And it felt so good to use my powers... and to be with a man again, and..." The tears began to fall as she waited for Abby to agree with her, to tell her that she was right to cut things off with Dave before they went any farther.

"Shannon Kelly, that is the silliest thing I've ever heard. It's been two years since Jason died. And you've said yourself he wouldn't want you to close yourself off. And I bet your brother would tell you the same thing."

"Oh Lord, please don't tell Chris anything about this." She covered her face with her hands. "He can be an overprotective bear when he thinks someone has hurt me. I certainly don't want him thinking Dave did anything wrong. Even I can admit this was all my fault. Dave didn't put on some big seduction act. It was all me."

"Can you please quit beating yourself up? You're a grown woman who just had sex with a very attractive, single, available man. What is wrong with that? No one cheated on anyone."

"Well, how about he's my partner at RPD, and there are rules about this kind of thing? And then there's the witchcraft."

Shannon had to stop as their waitress came to deliver their burgers.

"Oh, don't worry about Alice. She's one of us," Abby said as the girl set the plates in front of them.

"Sure am, and I hope to see you at the next coven meeting. Merry Meet," the waitress said cheerfully and headed back to the kitchen.

"Oh God, is everyone in this town a paranormal? How did I get mixed up with a place like this?"

"Well as to that, I think you were drawn here because of your abilities. And no, not everyone is a paranormal here. There are more non-para's, actually. I think it's about three-quarters N.P. to one- quarter para.

"Damn, girl, you're avoiding the subject, and you've got me off track and talking like a Chamber of Commerce brochure. The point is you're a witch. Dave is a witch. You two are obviously attracted to each other, and I just don't see that there is any problem here. From what I hear, Chief Anderson is now vouching for you in regards to these murders, and as soon as you go see Cassandra and get straight with the coven, things will be fine."

Shannon rolled her eyes. "I don't want to meet with the

head of the coven."

"High Priestess," Abby interjected.

"What?"

"The head of a coven is the high priestess or priest."

"Fine, whatever." Shannon rolled her eyes. "I don't want to be in the coven. I don't want to meet the High Priestess. What is she going to ask me, anyway? You have a great family history, all the way back to the Witch Trials. What have I got? A mom who practiced on the dark side and I…"

Shannon closed her mouth quickly.

"And you what?"

"I just don't want to talk to her."

"Cassandra isn't like that. She doesn't care about who your parents were. She's going to look at you and what you've done. That's all."

"That's what I'm afraid of," Shannon muttered.

Chapter 17

Conversation was stiff and stilted in the patrol car that evening. Dave was angry, Shannon embarrassed. Unfortunately, they had few calls, so there was nothing much to do for the first few hours except ride around silently fuming at each other. It was almost midnight when dispatch ordered them to the coroner's office to pick up a package from Dr. Lazard.

"Why is the coroner at work so late?" Shannon questioned. "Has something new happened I don't know about?"

"Lazard prefers to work at night; I told you he's a vampire, remember?"

"Oh, yeah." Shannon rolled her eyes. One more damn paranormal.

They pulled into the parking lot of the morgue, which was in the basement of the county hospital. The building was only a few years old. It had replaced a 1940s brick building in the downtown area and now was on its own campus out near the mall and the community college. Small maple trees dotted the lawn, still held in place with tree stakes. It would be beautiful someday, Shannon thought. But right now with only a few spring leaves on them, the trees reminded her of broomsticks sticking up toward the dark, night sky, giving the hospital a rather gloomy air.

"Hey, Dr. Lazard, we hear you have a package for Chief Anderson," Dave called out when they entered the morgue.

As the newest facility by far in the surrounding area, and with a coroner who had a national reputation, the county had sprung for all the latest equipment, hoping to bring in business from other, more rural areas nearby. There were refrigerated drawers along the back wall to hold bodies, several steel tables for autopsies, a lifting device, and an x-ray room. Dr. Lazard came out of the evidence room, removing his mask.

"Thanks for coming by," he said. He stripped off his latex gloves and held out his hand. He was dressed in his usual black jeans and button-down shirt, relieved only by his white medical coat. "Dave. Shannon, we meet again." He held out his hand after throwing his gloves in a trash can. "Y'all have saved me from having to stop by the police department before I head home."

"Is there anything new on the three Artificial Witch Murders?" Dave asked.

"Oh lord, please don't use the name the media has given them," Lazard said. "It's bad enough when people use it who don't know what they're talking about."

David winced, obviously feeling chastised by the doctor. "Sorry. I didn't mean anything by it. But when you keep hearing something…"

"No problem, Kid. I'm just feeling a bit petulant tonight."

Shannon started to chuckle as the doctor called Dave "kid" but quickly put her hand over her mouth and pretended to cough when she caught the scorching look her partner gave her.

"It's bad enough we have non-para's out there murdering young girls while they're fantasizing about being witches," Lazard went on, politely pretending not to notice Shannon's chuckle or the glower on Dave's face. "Now I've got para-on-para violence, too."

"What's going on?" Shannon asked.

"A couple of bobcats—feline shifters who live down by the river, *Cher*," he explained in an aside to Shannon. "They got into a fight two nights ago and really tore each other up. That's why I want you to hand-deliver these DNA samples to Captain Anderson. I don't like to put this kind of evidence on the internet. It can get hacked too easily."

"What about PackNet? Wouldn't that be safe? Even if it did get hacked, it wouldn't get out beyond the para community," Dave said.

"Call me old-fashioned, I just don't like these newfangled inventions."

Now it was Dave's turn to chuckle. "You better keep up, old man, or the world will pass you by." He gave Lazard a light punch to the shoulder.

"Will you two stop?" Shannon said. "There can't be that much age difference between you two. Although Dave does sometimes act like a child," she said, with an irritated glance at her partner.

"Thank you for the kind words, *Cher*, but I am older than I look."

Shannon gave him a questioning look.

"I migrated north from New Orleans shortly after the Louisiana Purchase. The city had become too crowded. I lived in a lot of places before I settled here. There were the descendants of the many French trappers who had immigrated south from Canada in this area. They spoke my language and were very welcoming."

Shannon's mouth was hanging open as she listened. "B...but that would make you..."

"I was born in 1697 in France; I wanted to see the world, so I left home when I was sixteen and found a berth on a ship to the New World. I quickly found that life at sea was not for me, and when I had the chance to disembark in Canada, I took it. I was lucky; I knew how to read and write, and so I got a job as a clerk with a shipping company. They sent me south, down the newly discovered Mississippi River, and there I used my skills to become the personal secretary for Jean-Baptiste Le Moyne de Bienville, the governor of New France and the Father of New Orleans."

"Over 300 years old," she finished in a whisper.

Lazard seemed not to hear her as he leaned back against the desk. He was lost in his memories.

"There were too many people. I had been there too long; people were starting to notice, so I left." He shrugged.

"How did you..." Shannon quickly shut her mouth when Dave nudged her.

"No no, *mon amie*," he said to David. "Don't worry; it doesn't bother me to talk about it. Particularly not when a beautiful woman is so interested in my story." He smiled and took her hand, leading her over to a desk chair. Dave glowered at them; Shannon pretended not to notice.

"You should have seen New Orleans back in those days. It already had the wild charm it has today. We saw the Spanish, the British, the Spanish again, and then Thomas Jefferson bought the entire region.

"Vampires come from France, you know. That is where we were first bred. Of course, they hid their nature, just as we do today. And although it was a time when superstitions were more often believed to be truth than today, that made it even more dangerous to be found out as a paranormal creature.

"But New Orleans, from its inception, was different. It attracted so many paranormal beings. The Loupe Garou, the voodoo priests and priestesses. They were all welcomed there.

I was very young, though, *Cher,* and I did not listen to the rumors. I went to a bar one evening and met a beautiful girl. I kept going back. She said she loved me. Soon I was spending every night I could with her. I wanted her to marry me. That night in bed she bit me, just a little nip. She drank my blood. A little at a time. I was hooked, as we say now. Soon I begged her to turn me. We would be together forever. That was all that she, or I, wanted."

"What happened? Why isn't she with you?"

"She was caught and killed, and I left New Orleans with a broken heart. I have never been back."

"Thank you so much for sharing your story, Dr. Lazard," Shannon said in a low voice.

"I told you the other day to call me Nathan. So few people call me by my first name here." He took her hand gently. "I wanted you to hear my story so that you will understand there can be new love when an old love dies."

Shannon stared into his eyes, fascinated.

Dave cleared his throat loudly. "Well, now that we have these samples I guess we should get them back to the station as soon as possible."

Shannon shook her head as if coming out of a trance. She glared at Dave, then turned back to the doctor.

"Thank you again, Nathan, for your thoughtfulness."

"It was my pleasure, *Cher*. If you ever need anything from me—even if just someone to talk to about loss and pain, you know where to find me."

Dave wanted this uncomfortable conversation over. He didn't want Shannon anywhere near the handsome Dr. Lazard. She had barely looked at him throughout their entire shift, and now she seemed fascinated by the damn vampire.

"We need to get back to headquarters," he said abruptly, then grabbed her elbow and hustled her back to the patrol car.

CHAPTER 18

"What the hell do you think you're doing, flirting with a vampire?" he said heatedly when they were back in their vehicle. "He's dangerous."

"What's your problem? I thought all you paranormal types stuck together," Shannon said, turning on the ignition.

"We protect each other from the non-paras because what is good for one is good for all. We respect each other. But we don't forget the nature of each paranormal we deal with. He's a vampire. He's not our kind. And given the chance, he'll enthrall you and turn you."

"'He's not our kind!' I can't believe you just said that. That is so prejudiced! Just because he's a vampire doesn't mean he wants to bite and turn everyone he sees."

"No, just the beautiful women," David said under his breath.

Shannon smiled sarcastically. "Why David, how sweet, I didn't know you thought I was beautiful."

"Didn't I show you last night?" he shot back at her.

She drew a deep breath. She'd enjoyed teasing him too much, and now she had gotten them right back to what had started this fight in the first place—the fact that they had slept together.

"Look, let's call a truce. I'm not sorry I slept with you," David broke into her thoughts. "I'm not going to tell you that because it's just not true. I enjoyed every moment. I'm only sorry that it seems to have ruined our friendship. Can we go back to the way it was?"

He looked so sincere that Shannon had to give in. "Okay, it's my fault not yours. It was my first time since... since Jason..." She took a deep breath, closed her eyes for a moment, and continued. "I took it out on you, and that wasn't fair." She held out her hand. "So truce?"

"Truce," he replied, shaking it. Maybe he did hold it a little too long. Maybe he did notice how soft her skin was. So sue him. He was only a witch, not Superman.

If Shannon thought that this new truce meant that she could go back to ignoring her powers, it didn't take long to realize that just wasn't going to be possible in Rivelou. Dawn was breaking when they delivered the coroner's package to Chief Anderson a short time later; he made it a point to stop and ask how the witchcraft lesson had gone.

"It was fine, sir. I'm glad to understand I was wrong in thinking all witches and witchcraft were the same as my mother." She hoped that showing that she had tried would be enough.

They all walked out to the hallway as the chief continued speaking. "Good, good. Then you and Dave will be keeping up with the lessons. I'm glad to hear that. You couldn't have a better teacher." He slapped David on the back. "You seem to be impressing all the right people, Shannon. Dr. Lazard called me after you left his office; he wanted to make sure you were no longer on the suspect list. Said it was obvious you could not be a part of anything like that and you were going to make a fine addition to the force. Dave, we need to make sure she's introduced to Cassandra as soon as possible, also."

"Of course, sir, I'll look into it."

Dave opened the door of the locker room and put his hand on Shannon arm, turning her toward him. "See, I told you everything would be fine with the chief.

At that moment another officer, Devon Li, walked up behind them. The young woman was tall, willowy, and athletic looking, with straight black hair and almond-shaped brown eyes. In short, she was the exact opposite of Shannon and had always made her feel a little inadequate.

"Sucking up to everyone in town now, are we, Shannon?" Devon asked sarcastically. She made a show of noticing David's hand resting on Shannon's arm. "Dave, the chief, *and* Dr. Lazard? Maybe I should just say sucking them."

"What the hell, Devon? Shannon's done nothing to…"

"That's right. Shannon's done nothing. She just walks around batting those baby blues, and everyone in Rivelou, from the Betrand family, to you, to the chief, and now Nathan Lazard bend over backward to make sure things go smoothly for her.

Why is that, I wonder?"

"You don't know what you're talking about!"

Shannon put a hand on her partner's arm. "I can fight my own battles, David." She turned to the other woman. With her magic newly awakened, she sensed that Devon was a non-para, and it didn't take any special powers to understand that Devon was jealous of what she thought was a relationship with her partner. "Don't take me on, bitch. I can and will take you." With that, she turned around and swept out of the door, not bothering to change her clothes..

Dave stared after her. "Wow. That was hot. I think I'm in love," he mumbled, forgetting that Devon could hear him. When he looked over at her, he was almost sure he could see smoke coming from her ears. Well, it couldn't be helped. Devon was a bridge he had burned long ago.

He hurried into the locker room to finish changing his own clothes, then rushed out to catch his partner, but she was already gunning her car out of the parking lot. Well, he figured he could give her until lunchtime to get over it.

CHAPTER 19

Shannon was making a sandwich for herself when she heard a motorcycle pull into her driveway. "Damnit," she thought. "Doesn't he ever quit?"

Dave didn't bother to knock on the front door; he just came around through the garden and entered her kitchen.

"Didn't your mother teach you to knock?"

"Nope," he said, grabbing a couple of chips from the bag on the table. "Can you make me one of those? I didn't have time to grab lunch." He pointed to the sandwich in process on her cutting board. "A little bit of mayo, no mustard please."

"Well since you asked so nicely." She grabbed the bread bag and slammed a few slices on the counter. "Ham or corned beef?"

"How about both. Maybe some of that Swiss, too." He grinned at her.

"So why are you here interrupting my free time?" Shannon asked, trying very hard not to grin. Why was it so difficult to stay angry at the man? And why did he have to look so delicious sitting in her kitchen with his bad boy grin. She banged the plate with his sandwich in front of him, trying hard not to smile back at him.

"You heard the chief. We need to keep up your lessons."

"I took that as a suggestion, not a demand." Shannon finished preparing her own sandwich and sat down at the table across from him.

"Wow, girl, forget the witchcraft. You need to work on your listening skills. Anderson does not suggest. He orders."

"Yeah, I really knew that. I was just hoping." Her corned beef and Swiss had suddenly turned to sawdust in her mouth.

"No such luck. So, I brought my supplies with me this time since I figured you wouldn't have everything we need here." He picked up the backpack he'd left on her floor when he came in and, opening it, took out candles, crystals, a couple of copper bowls, and a pouch of salt, and laid them in front of her on the table.

"Do you have a good room for us to use? Some place where we can make a protection circle and not have any distractions?"

Shannon sighed. Obviously she wasn't going to get out of this. "Yeah, Ana and I just finished painting one of the upstairs bedrooms the other day. I don't even have the furniture back in it yet."

"Perfect."

~~~

Learning to use her powers once again was exhausting. Maybe that was what was getting to her, she thought. She had to consciously undo bad habits and ways of doing things that came from the dark side of her power rather than the light. Watching Dave's tattoos glow to life on his chest once again, she said, "Tell me about your tattoos. How do they help you when you're working a spell? Should I get some? Will they make learning this stuff again easier for me?"

Dave took a breath as he pictured Shannon glowing with magical light across her body. It would be beautiful. He shook the image from his head and answered her question.

"There are a lot of reasons witches get tattoos. First, for protection. They can ward off evil spirits, even evil thoughts emanating toward you from someone else. They can help with healing as well as help us to focus our magic. And yes, when you are ready to totally accept your power, I think you should get some. I'll help you figure out what would work best for you. But you don't need to rush into it; first things first."

They returned to their practice and after another hour she was wiped out. Dave called a halt for the day. "I don't want you so exhausted you have to call off shift tonight," he told her. "That might leave me partnering with Devon."

"What is it with that girl? She's been after me for months. Always a snide comment or something just this side of insulting to say. But she was over the top today."

"It's not you. You didn't do anything. She's just a bitch."

"Yeah, but she never seemed to notice me until I

partnered with you. Oh wait... Dave the Player. I can't believe you were attracted to Devon."

Dave had the grace to blush.

"Well, you know when she first came on the force, we were kind of the only ones our age here. Everyone was older, and we just sort of bonded."

"Like superglue, apparently. So what unstuck you?"

"She was jealous and possessive. I just wanted a good time..."

Shannon rolled her eyes and muttered, "Of course you did."

"...and she wanted things to go a lot farther. She's N.P.., and it was just too hard to try to have a relationship with her. There were too many things I couldn't share."

Strangely, Dave's words made Shannon feel better about her own night with Dave. If he'd had sex with Devon of all people, obviously he really was the playboy she had accused him of being. She hadn't mortally wounded him by rejecting him. He was probably already over her.

"I've got some leftovers we can have before we head into work," she said as they walked downstairs. "It'll save you having to go all the way back to your place."

"Sure, thanks, if it's not any problem."

Shannon pulled the leftovers out of the fridge as Dave got out the silverware and plates. He noticed a book she had left on the counter. *"Witchcraft: A Guide for Beginners,"* he read. "Shannon, I can't believe you're reading this trash. It's a bunch of nonsense."

Shannon blushed. She'd meant to get rid of the book a couple of days ago. "That's what Abby said when she looked at it. I just bought it because her friend with the new store next door to hers seemed to really need sales. I never thought it had anything to do with real witchcraft."

"What new store?"

"It's next door to The Wolf's Den. It's called Baubles and Beads. I guess that's why you never noticed it. It's only been open a week or so, and it's got a real girl vibe. Not your kind of place; no hubcaps or radiators," she teased.

"This doesn't look like 'girl vibe' stuff."

"Oh you know, she's trying for a 'supernatural flair.'" Shannon used air quotes as she said the words. "But it's really all just crystals and candles to draw people in so they'll look at the expensive stuff she really hopes to sell."

Dave slowly put the book down on the table. "A supernatural flair?"

"Yeah, you know. Along with the other stuff she has Tarot cards, Ouija boards, a bunch of other stuff people think they need to be a real witch." Shannon wasn't really paying attention to the conversation as she put the food on the table. Finally she looked at Dave and noticed his expression. "What is it?"

"We've been saying these 'Artificial Witch Murders' look like the work of someone who wants to be a witch but isn't—someone who knows just a little bit but not enough. Like the stuff in this book," he tapped the book lying on the table between them. "Who is this woman? Do you know anything about her?"

"It's a couple. Her name is Salvia, and his is Harrison. They seemed like an odd pair, but that's about all I can tell you. I think Abby know more."

"Maybe we should go check them out. I'd like to get more of a feel for them before I talk to the chief or anyone else about this. And I'm really starting to think we need to tell the chief about them. Do you have anything else you have to do before work? Maybe we can stop over there on our way."

CHAPTER 20

"Before we go talk with Salvia and Harrison, I think we need to have a chat with Winnie," Shannon said as they met in the parking lot of the shopping area where both Salvia's and Abby's stores were located. Dave had ridden his Harley while Shannon had driven over in her car so they could go straight from here to work.

"I really don't see why you feel the need to talk to Winnie; she's still distressed about her friend being murdered," Dave said. "I don't want to upset her more."

"Well, first because I think she might know something." Shannon leaned against the side of her car; she had a feeling this might be a long conversation.

"But…"

Shannon held up her hand to stop David. "I'm not saying she's involved in any way in the murders, or that she's even done anything wrong. But she grew up with the girl; they went to the same school, had classes together, knew a lot of the same people. She very well may have seen something or heard something and not even have realized at the time that it was suspicious. And you know that if this were anyone except your cousin, you'd be the first one to want to question her."

Dave drew in a deep breath. "I want to argue with you, but I can't. You're right. And look, you haven't even had to remind me that I said you could talk to Winnie after you started working on your powers."

"Great. Let's go. And I won't even remind you that I've now had two lessons, not just one."

They headed into The Wolf's Den and found Abby alone behind her counter.

"Hey Abby, is Winnie working today?" Dave asked.

"Yeah, she's in the back. But what did you need her for?" Abby asked, noticing their serious expressions. "I hope it's not more bad news. She's really distraught about her friend's death."

Abby turned around and called into the back room. "Winnie, your cousin is out here."

Winnie walked out with a smile. "Hi Dave, what are you doing here?" She stopped suddenly when she saw Shannon. "Why is she here?"

"Winnie, she's my partner. Don't talk to her like that."

Winnie looked embarrassed. "Sorry," she mumbled.

"No problem, Winnie," Shannon said. "We just wanted to talk to you a bit more about your friend, Ashley."

Winnie's face crumbled and her eyes filled with tears. "That's just it, you know. She wasn't really my friend. Not anymore. And that was my fault."

"How so?" asked Shannon. She gave Dave a pointed look when he started to step in the moment his cousin seemed upset.

"Ashley needed to be special. From the time I met her in middle school, she always had to be the best at everything. And usually she was. She got the best grades, was great in sports. She even could sing, too. She was always the lead in the school plays. And she always bragged about it. I guess that's why Kenzy and Willow and I told her. We just got tired of her always bragging about being the best at everything. We wanted her to know we could do something she never could."

"So you told her you all were witches," Shannon confirmed.

"We did more than that. She didn't believe us at first when we said it, so we showed her some things. Like making fire and calling up the wind."

When Winnie mentioned fire Shannon looked pointedly at Dave. It hadn't been too many days since he'd scared her with that same little trick and almost made her crash the patrol car.

Dave ignored the look and ran his hand over his beard. "Winnie, you've known since first grade never to talk. All of you have!" he exclaimed in frustration.

Abby put her arm around the girl. "Dave, don't chastise her. She was young. They all were. And it's done now, and she and her friends have all learned that lesson in the hardest way possible."

"I know. I'm sorry, I yelled at you, Winnie."

She came out from behind the counter to give him a hug. "I know, Dave, and don't worry. I deserved to be yelled at. What we did was wrong. And it made Ashley afraid of us. She never wanted to hang around with any of us after that."

"All right, Winnie, your telling Ashley about your powers back in middle school may or may not have had anything to do with her murder." Shannon wanted to get the conversation back on track. "What's important now is what you may have seen or heard in the last few weeks that could help us find whoever did this to Ashley and the other two girls. Tell us more about this semester. I understand you were in a class with her?"

"Okay, but I don't think I know anything important, except maybe…"

"What, Winnie? Have you remembered something?"

"Yeah, there was something. We were both in Biz 101. It's an auditorium class. And when we came in the first day, and there were so many people there, we saw each other. We haven't been close for a few years, like I said, but it was just good to know someone, you know? And we started sitting together. She never mentioned anything about powers or witchcraft though. I kind of figured she'd forgotten about it or had decided she'd imagined it.

"But then about a month ago she said something. I didn't pay much attention at the time, just figured she was up to her usual bragging again."

"What did she say?" Shannon asked.

"She told me she was going to learn witchcraft and be a more powerful witch than I ever could be."

"That's great, Winnie. That could be really important," Shannon said. "What else do you remember? Did she say how she was going to get these powers? Or who was going to teach her?"

"No," Winnie shook her head. "That's all she said. And I didn't pay too much attention. There's no way someone without power can get it, so I just figured she was bragging like she always had."

They questioned Winnie some more, but that was all

she knew. Finally Dave said, "It's getting late. If we're going to check out next door, we need to go now or we'll be late for work. Abby, Winnie, thanks for the help. We'll tell you if we find out anything."

CHAPTER 21

"I need a gift for Ana and Chris for their engagement party next week. That can be our excuse for stopping in. I'm not sure, but Harrison looks like a biker to me. I bet that's his." She pointed to the far corner of the lot where a Ducati Monster Plus stood. "Maybe you can bring up your bike as a way to strike up a conversation while I'm talking to Salvia."

"Yeah, nice bike; sounds like a plan. I'll kind of wander around and see if I can find out anything interesting while you shop. If this Harrison guy comes up to me, maybe I can use that as a way to start a conversation."

There was no one in the front of the store when they first entered, but they could make out raised voices in the back room. As the door chime tinkled, the voices stopped, and Salvia quickly came out to greet them. Dave sneezed as the overwhelming smell of patchouli mixed with the distinctive tang of marijuana tickled his nose.

"Oh, hello again, Salvia," Shannon said. "I was telling my friend David about your cute store. We need to get some gifts for an engagement party this weekend, and I thought this might be the perfect place."

"I'm so glad you came back. I'm sure we can find something perfect. Why don't you tell me a little bit about the couple? I know I can help you find the perfect gift."

"It's my brother and his fiancée," Shannon started to explain, glancing at the merchandise in a leisurely fashion as David wandered away.

He had made his way over to the bookshelf near the back of the store and began browsing the varied selection of books and other items when a man came out of the back room. He was wiping his hands on a towel as if he had just finished washing up.

"Interesting collection of books you have here," Dave said, picking one up at random. He assumed from Shannon's description that this was Harrison. The man wore leather biker pants and a t-shirt which showed off his tattooed arms.

"Oh, I don't know too much about them. The store is Salvia's baby," he said. "You know how it is; got to keep the old lady happy."

Dave chuckled. "If Shannon ever heard me call her my 'old lady' she'd have my head—or maybe some other parts of my anatomy I value even more." Harrison obviously assumed they were a couple, and that worked for Dave on several levels. "Looks like you all are into the paranormal." He got the conversation on the track he wanted as he pointed toward the books on the shelves.

"Yeah, that's Salvia again. She's really into all this supernatural witchcraft stuff. Now I'm more of a live and let live kind of guy, you know? Whatever you want to believe is good with me. I don't really care."

This had been easier than Dave had thought. They'd skipped over bonding over motorcycles or tattoos and gone straight to Salvia's interest in witchcraft.

"This looks interesting." Dave picked up a book, *"Rituals, Spells, and Charms,"* he read the title aloud as he flipped through the pages. Finding it rather innocuous, he moved on down the row toward the back of the shop. He noticed that the subject matter of the covers became darker and more explicit as he went.

"Necromancy," he read. "You don't believe in talking to the dead, do you?" He allowed a lot of skepticism to enter his voice.

"I told you; it's not me, man. It's all Salvia. She likes to read a lot of different things. Crystals now, that's something I can get into. The stones are pretty whether you believe they have power or not, and some of them have good monetary value."

He subtly tried to move Dave away from the books and head him toward the shelf with the crystals, but Dave ignored him. He kept perusing the books, reading the titles out loud. *"Raising Demons,"* he read. "Hm, that could be kind of cool. *Curses and How to Break Them;* yeah, I guess if you're going to curse someone, you'd better know how to take it off if you need to—or in case someone curses you in return." He tried to sound as if he were intrigued by the titles even though his skin crawled at the thought of someone untrained accidentally using the instructions in this particular book. Not every book on the shelves was filled with fakery. There were some powerful spells written in some of them he realized as he glanced through several, including the book on curses. Maybe he should get it and ask Shannon if this were the kind of thing her mother had been into. Or maybe not. Shannon's mother was still a touchy subject with her. He was just barely back in her good graces again.

"Yeah, I know what you mean. I tried to tell Salvia that maybe some of this stuff wasn't appropriate or should at least be put in the back room where kids can't see it, but she wasn't having it."

"She's really into curses and stuff, huh?" Again, he made sure he sounded skeptical. He could feel Harrison's discomfort—and something else. Dave reached out carefully with his own power. Yes. There it was. The man definitely had some power of his own. Dave couldn't identify exactly what type of paranormal Harrison was right away. In fact, he decided, opening his senses even more as Harrison didn't react to his probing, Dave didn't think the man was aware of his power at all.

There were plenty of people like that in the non-para world. Often, they were untrained, and came from a family background that did not acknowledge magic or thought of their powers only as "being lucky," or "having good intuition."

But the conversation, or Dave's probing, was making Harrison nervous. Dave decided it would be better to back off and change the subject. "Hey, is that Ducati in the back of the lot yours?" he asked. He kept the book on curses in his hand as if he had forgotten he was holding it as they walked toward the front of the shop, discussing the advantages of Dave's Harley versus Harrison's Ducati as they went.

CHAPTER 22

Over in the front corner of the store, Salvia and Shannon were looking at copper and crystal bowls when Shannon noticed a beautiful walnut tray with a silhouette of wolves in the moonlight hand carved in the center.

"Oh, this is perfect," she said. "Now let me see what else might go with it. Maybe a cheese knife?"

At that moment, David walked up carrying a book in his hand.

"What have you found, Honey?" he asked, putting his arm around her. Shannon stiffened, then remembered they were undercover. She'd called him, "her friend," when they came in the store, but she was going to assume that it had been useful to give Harrison the idea that they were together. At least, she'd go with that assumption until she found out otherwise. If she discovered that wasn't the case, she'd have a few choice words for him later.

But as she leaned into him in her new role of girlfriend, she found herself relaxing, as if his arms represented safety. She felt as if her body were betraying her; she was used to being on her own. She didn't want to depend on a man who might decide to leave—or be taken away from her. Right now, though, she reminded herself she had to keep up the act.

"I'm thinking Ana would like this tray," she said, showing it to Dave.

"Yeah, I'm sure she would. But what about your brother? Aren't you going to get something for him, too?"

"You don't believe Chris would like the tray? You think men can't want to entertain with nice things?"

"I think your guy looks more like a beer-cans-and-bags-of-chips kind of entertainer," Salvia said as she looked appreciatively at Dave, who was dressed in torn jeans and a T-shirt that showed off his muscular physique. The move raised Shannon's hackles, and she stepped a little closer to Dave, putting her arm around his waist. Forget about her discomfort. And no, she told herself, she was not jealous. This was all just part of the act for their impromptu undercover foray.

Both Salvia and Dave noticed the gesture. Dave looked down at her with a grin, then proceeded to kiss her hair. Shannon gave her partner a little pinch.

"Uh uh uh," he whispered softly in her ear. "Remember we're a loving couple."

Her smile may have been more of an angry smirk than a loving glance. Salvia must have noticed also; she seemed to think she might be losing a sale. "Harrison, why don't you come ring up this tray for Shannon?" she called. "Oh, and did you want the book?" she asked Dave, noticing it in his hand.

"Yeah, maybe, it looks kind of cool."

"What did you find?" Shannon reached for the book as an excuse to move away from Dave's embrace.

He held out the book for her to see.

"Curses? Really, Dave? Who do you want to curse?" Shannon was back in her undercover role, trying to show amused interest rather than the deep revulsion she felt as she looked at the book. It reminded her too much of the witchcraft her mother had practiced.

"Maybe I could curse Devon for you?" Dave joked.

"Hmm, now that's not a bad idea."

"Are you interested in witchcraft?" Salvia asked as Harrison took the tray and began to wrap it for them.

"Oh, I don't know…" She decided playing hard to get would seem more believable to Salvia than being too enthusiastic right away.

"Shannon, you know you've always said you were interested in this sort of thing," said Dave persuasively.

"If you are truly interested in the supernatural, I have a group that meets on Wednesday nights to explore the topic," Salvia said.

"Really," said Dave. "We'd love to come."

"Sorry, Dude," Harrison said as he began to ring up their purchase. "The group's only for women." He rolled his eyes subtly at David, expressing his skepticism. "Hey, did you decide if you're going to buy the book?"

Dave held it out. "Yeah, I guess we'll get this, too. I think Shannon's brother will get a kick out of it."

"Harrison's right. My Wednesday group is a women's empowerment meeting, no men allowed. I'm sure you could get a lot of benefit from it, Shannon. The group is all about opening ourselves to the universe and developing our power. There are several spiritual seekers in the group who I'm sure you would enjoy meeting."

"Babe, really, you should try it. It sounds interesting," Dave said.

"Well, what could it hurt? I can always come one time and see if I like it. How many other women are in the group?"

"We recently lost a member. Right now, we have twelve; you'd be our lucky number thirteen."

After they paid for their purchases and headed outside, Winnie came out of The Wolf's Den and ran up to them as they headed for their vehicles.

"Hey, Cuz, did you think of something else?" Dave asked her.

"No, not really. I just wondered if you'd learned anything more about Ashley's murder when you visited the other store."

"You know I can't tell you anything about an ongoing investigation. Let me know if you have any clues for finding the killer."

"Wow! You sound just like the cops on *Law and Order*."

David laughed, noticing that Abby had come out of the store also and was listening just as closely as Winnie to what he had to say.

"But you do have something, anything, you can tell us about, don't you? Something more than is on the local news?" she asked. "Everyone in town is worried—the non-paras just as much as the paranormals."

"Abby, Dave told you, we can't talk about anything we know." Shannon stepped into the conversation.

"Damn it's frustrating that you two are such law-abiding police officers," Abby said with a grin. "But hey, let's talk about something more pleasant before you go. Ana and Chris's engagement party is coming up this Friday night, and I see you have a package in your hand."

"I just bought them a cool gift at Salvia's store. It's all wrapped, or I'd show it to you."

"You're invited, Abby? What about me? Now that I've helped you buy the gift, not to mention that 'really cool' gift for Chris, I think you should take me to the party with you," Dave said, trying to sound as if he were joking. He would love an excuse to spend more off-duty time with Shannon.

She just rolled her eyes.

"Well, if she won't bring you as her date, I'm going, so I will," said Abby. "I've known Ana for years. She likes to stop in here when she's picking up groceries."

Shannon found herself bristling at the idea of Abby taking Dave to the party even though she knew it made no sense. She didn't want him, after all, so it was perfectly fine for Abby to be interested. Still, she added quickly, "Dave, you can come with me. I'd love to have someone with me so everyone doesn't get on my case about not having a date. Ana's grandmother Ida is absolutely dying to match me up with someone—anyone."

"Yeah, I know how you feel. Dave, can we share you? That will keep Ida guessing," Abby joked. "And by the way, did you see anything else you thought they would like over at Baubles and Beads? I need to get a gift, too."

"Oh, they have lots of beautiful things," Shannon said. "But what about bringing them something from your own store?"

"That feels like cheating," Abby laughed. "It doesn't count unless I've actually gone shopping for it. And by the way, Dave, what did you think of Salvia and Harrison?"

"They're interesting," he answered cautiously.

"I hear Salvia's doing a women's empowerment group on Wednesday nights," Winnie said. "I was thinking of going."

"Winnie, I don't want you anywhere near that group!" Dave's voice rose a notch at the thought of his cousin getting involved with the woman he was beginning to think of as the prime suspect in the Artificial Witch Murders.

"Dave, that's really a bit controlling, don't you think?" asked Abby.

"Dave's right. No one needs to go over there," said Shannon.

Winnie and Abby exchanged looks. "So, you think Salvia and Harrison do have something to do with the murders?" Winnie asked.

"We didn't say that. I told you we can't say anything about the investigation. Just stay away from them. I mean it. It's for your own good," said Dave.

As Winnie started to argue with her cousin, Shannon stepped in. "Dave, we need to get to work or we're going to be late." She pushed her partner toward his motorcycle, turning as she got to the door of her own car to give an apologetic look to the two women. "I'll talk to you soon," she mouthed silently.

Fifteen minutes later they were heading into the department. "We have to tell Chief Anderson what we found out," she said.

"Yeah, I'm not sure how he's going to feel about us and our little undercover gig. You signing up for these 'empowerment classes' could be dangerous, you know, if what we suspect is right. The chief may want to send in a more experienced detective."

"But I've already got the in. The chief can't tell me what to do on my own time. I'm going to do this, Dave, whether he likes it or not."

CHAPTER 23

The chief hadn't liked it when Shannon and Dave told him of their "shopping excursion" at Baubles and Beads, their encounter with Salvia and Harrison, as well as their suspicions about the pair. Their announcement resulted in a rather noisy meeting with the Chief, Tony Abello, and Jake Waseaux, the two detectives who were working the case.

"I might have expected something like this from her," Tony said, pointing his finger at Shannon. "She's hasn't been a team player since she arrived here. But you, Thorne. I trained you. You know better than this."

"Now that's not fair…" Dave started when Shannon cut in.

"I am a team player; you all just never told me the rules of the game…"

"All right, all right. Settle down," Chief Anderson made a lowering motion with his hands. "Everyone, settle down and sit down. We may not like the way these two officers have gone about it, but the fact is they have come up with a substantial lead. Something we've been sorely short on in this case. Now how are we going to handle it?"

His question started an eruption of comments from everyone in the office again.

"She's not experienced in undercover work. And the last time she went rogue, and she and her husband tried to do something off book, it got him killed," said Jake.

Shannon felt as if someone had taken all the air out of her body. That's what they thought of her here in Rivelou? Her fellow officers thought she was responsible for Jason's death?

"That is totally unfair," Dave jumped to her defense. "You don't have all the facts."

"And you do?"

"Yeah, she's told me about it. I'm her partner."

"Well, she needs to learn to work with people other than

just you, Dave."

Again, Chief Johnson stepped in.

"Quiet down. Now!" He used his siren's voice to quell the disruption, and everyone in the room found themselves suddenly sitting in the chairs around the table with their hands folded in front of them like old-time school children.

"I don't want anyone else speaking unless I give you express permission—and don't make me have to compel you again, do you understand me?" They all nodded obediently. "Now Shannon, you've met this pair more than once. Tell us your impressions of them."

Shannon thought back to the times she'd been in the store and spoken with Salvia and Harrison.

"Salvia is definitely the one in charge. Harrison defers to her. Even when he disagrees with her. He looks like a tough biker dude, with his tattoos and the way he dresses, but I don't think that's who he is at heart. I think Salvia can get him to do anything, whether he wants to or not. And it's not some paranormal power she's using on him, either. I think he's in love with her, and it's got him blindly following her. Or maybe it's just his personality; he's a follower, not a leader."

"So exactly what makes you think they're involved in these murders? I want more details this time; anything you can think of. We need more than just suspicions here."

"It's something about the way Salvia speaks about things—not that she's said anything about the murders, you understand. It's that you can tell she wants power—paranormal power—and she thinks if she learns enough about witchcraft and can recite enough spells, she will have it.

"On top of that, somehow, even without power of her own, she has picked up on the fact that Harrison does have it. Maybe she's seen him do things, or 'see' things, without him even realizing what it is he is doing. I don't know; I'm not really sure exactly what type of paranormal he is—maybe Dave has more of an idea." She looked over at him questioningly, and he just shrugged, so she continued.

"But, anyway, I think Salvia is jealous of Harrison's abilities. Even though Harrison doesn't admit his power even to himself—and I guess I know something about that," she added with a half-smile and a shrug, admitting that she had been doing the same thing until recently.

"Anyway, she believes that Harrison can foresee stuff. She told me he has the sight." She paused. "No, that's not how she put it. She said, 'Harrison can see the future.' It embarrassed him when she said it, whether it's true or not."

"And then there is this 'empowerment group,' of hers," Dave added. "It just feels shady —the way she said they had lost a member recently, and Shannon would be the 'lucky number thirteen.' That's when I really felt we were on the right track."

"Do they know you're cops?" asked Tony.

"I don't know." Shannon thought back to her encounters with the pair. "I've always been off duty when I've been in the shop, but we did stop by Abby's store the other day when we were both in uniform."

"I was checking on my cousin. She was friends with Ashley Butler, the last girl who was killed," Dave added.

"So, here's what we have," said the chief, ticking off the points on his fingers. "A woman who wants to be a witch but has no power. Her partner does, and she is jealous of it. And she is starting a group that sounds suspiciously like a coven. It sounds thin, and it's not as if we can get a search warrant for their store or their home with just this. I don't think we need one at this point anyway, but it does give us a place to start.

"Shannon, I'm going to let you investigate this further. But you are to wear a wire and be in touch with Dave or one of the other people on this team anytime you are with these people. No more off the book activity here, either of you." He paused and looked sternly at Shannon and then David. "If what you think is true, this is a very dangerous group. And one more thing—do not tell anyone else about this. Not your family, not coworkers. Nothing goes beyond the five of us. We know there are eleven other people in this group, and we don't know who they are or how involved they are."

Shannon could hardly contain her excitement as they left the chief's office. She was finally being listened to and was going to be allowed to go undercover. She was practically bouncing with enthusiasm as she and Dave headed to their patrol car to start their shift.

"I can't believe the chief listened to us. And he's going to let me do this!"

Dave wasn't as excited. "I know, and I'm glad you feel like they're listening to you. But Shannon, when we were talking to the Chief and Tony and Jake, it hit me just how dangerous this is. I'm worried about you. Don't do anything stupid, okay?"

"I would never do anything stupid. I'm going to do exactly what the chief says. I won't even fuss about you giving me more witchcraft lessons. I know I need every advantage I can get. And I know you'll have my back the whole time."

"Of course," Dave said. Yes, he'd have her back at work—and he wanted more, also. He pictured her as she had looked when they made love, smiling up at him. He wanted that again, and again. He was in love with Shannon Kelly. Now he just had to be patient until she was ready to return his feelings.

CHAPTER 24

Saturday morning found Shannon busy helping Ana's grandmother, mother, and sister decorate the farmhouse that was not only the Betrand family homestead, but the headquarters for the Rivelou shifter pack. It was also where Chris and Ana's engagement party would be held later that day. The men were cleaning out the barn for dancing and setting up tables and chairs on the lawn for dinner while the women decorated everything with a moon-and-stars theme. "Ana has so many non-para friends, we needed to be subtle with the décor," her sister Channing explained. "No wolves and pentagrams for this party."

"I'm just so happy to see Ana marrying a good man," said Ana's grandmother, Ida.

"But couldn't she have chosen a wolf this time?" Donna, Ana's mother, complained.

"She's never been conventional. She was never going to marry someone you and Daddy wanted—no offense, Shannon," said Channing.

"None taken. I wasn't exactly thrilled when my brother started dating a shapeshifter, particularly a wolf," Shannon confessed.

Donna gave her a glare that could have peeled paint. Obviously, in Donna's mind it was fine for her to disparage her daughter's prospective in-laws. The same obviously didn't hold true when the prospective in-laws voiced reservations about her daughter. Oh well, considering what her mother would have done to any boyfriends Shannon had brought home, she guessed she could understand Donna's feelings. Her mother wouldn't just have criticized the boyfriends; Shannon would have been lucky if she had *only* turned them into a toad.

Ida gave Ana a sympathetic glance. She'd been dealing with her daughter-in-law for a lot longer than Shannon had. "What about you, Channing?" Ida asked now, with a mischievous smile. "Are you seeing anyone?"

Channing blushed bright red. "I'll take that as a yes," her grandmother laughed.

"Well, who is it? I hope you've picked a shifter—and a wolf at that. We want to keep our bloodline strong," said Donna. "When your grandfather retires and your father is the head of the pack, he's not going to put up with a lot of this intermarriage nonsense."

Shannon caught a look between Ida and Channing. Apparently, Donna noticed it too. "What are you two making faces about? You know it's true. Remy thinks there's too much intermarriage allowed; we need to keep the bloodlines true if we're going to continue to be dominant in this world."

"Donna, that's what you think; I'm not sure my son agrees with you," Ida said.

"And Mom, are you sure Dad wants to take over the pack?" Channing asked gently. "He's always been much more interested in running Bertrand Enterprises than in being the pack Alpha."

Bertrand Enterprises was the business arm of the pack. The company managed the farm and several other businesses in the area, including an outdoor adventure company and a craft brewery, among other pack-owned businesses. Remy handled the pack's relationships with the non-para's, something he very much enjoyed. Dan currently worked with his father as head of public relations for the company.

"Of course he plans to take over the pack. It's his birthright. He's had to find something to do while his father was still pack leader, that's all. Frankly, I never expected Hank to last this long," Donna replied rather tactlessly.

Shannon studiously arranged white candles on the tables, then scattered gold confetti stars around them, making a great show of paying attention to the work she was doing while trying to catch every bit of the family drama playing out in front of her. "Chris needs to know this; he's marrying into this family," she told herself; it was as good an excuse as any for gathering the gossip. Of course, if she knew her brother, he already had a better handle on the Bertrand pack's politics than she ever would.

Ida was ignoring the fact that her daughter-in-law had just

predicted that her husband might die at any moment. "Yes, Donna, leading the pack could be considered Remy's birthright, but you know full well that's not how it works, and really never was. He has to prove himself the strongest, most savvy in the pack to become the leader. Thank goodness Hank has gotten us away from the medieval practices of the past—it's no longer a fight to the death to take over a pack. At least not here in Rivelou, even if some of the other packs are still stuck in their medieval ways."

"Oh? I didn't know that," said Shannon, giving up on pretending not to listen. "What is the procedure?"

"Of course, we still have tests of strength and fighting ability," Channing said. "But at least here in Rivelou there is no fight to the death. When the pack leader is ready to step down— or if a majority of the pack wants a new leader—everyone is called together, and there is a request for nominations. A person can nominate himself, or he can be nominated by others. After the various tests are finished, as well as a good bit of lobbying by each candidate's supporters—the pack votes on the wolf they want to lead them."

"So, you see, it's about much more than just physical ability," put in Ida. "We want what we have developed here in Rivelou to continue. We want a peaceful life where we don't have to worry about our husbands and fathers and sons being killed at any moment and we want to make sure we are led by the best person, not just the one who is best at killing."

"But not every pack thinks the same," said Donna. "There are plenty of them out there who would be happy to come in and take over this territory, like those McTier's from near Louisville. They'd be in here running everything as soon as they sniffed the first sign of a weakness. That's why the pack leader always has to be strong, vigilant, and on guard. An elderly leader who no longer is in his prime is ripe to have the pack stolen from him."

Donna seemed a little too happy at this idea, Shannon thought. And Channing suddenly busied herself with checking the plates and cutlery on the buffet table. When Shannon tried to catch her eye, she just looked away.

"I know you've always wanted to be the pack mother, but

I'm not sure that's what my son wants." Ida continued the conversation with Donna. "He's never liked to be in the spotlight, and he's never enjoyed the politicking that goes along with it either. And remember, it is also Danny's birthright. He's interested in leading and already is much more involved in running the business of the pack than Remy ever has been."

When Donna started to argue back, Channing turned from the buffet table and stepped in quickly to change the subject. "Shannon, is there any word on the murders of those three poor girls?"

"We have some leads," Shannon said cautiously. She understood Channing's desire to get her mother away from what had become an extremely awkward conversation, but she didn't want to give too much away about the murder investigation, either.

"Your brother should be working on this case," Donna now declared. "Isn't Chris supposed to be some kind of expert at tracking these types of crimes down?"

"We don't believe the murders are being committed by a paranormal. He and my partner, Dave Thorne, were instrumental in helping to figure that out. So, since it doesn't involve a paranormal, Chris isn't part of the investigation anymore. It's strictly a police matter."

Chris's role as a Hunter had changed over the past year as he had gained acceptance with Hank, Ana's grandfather and the pack Alpha, as well as with Chief Anderson. He was now an unofficial liaison to the Rivelou Police Department, handling any paranormal matters that could not easily be taken care of by the police without bringing too much attention from the non-para world.

Hank had also endorsed him as a watchman or guardian for the paranormal world, putting it out on PackNet that Chris was to be trusted to hunt only paranormals who had broken the law of a pack or coven. It was a relief to Shannon. She felt Chris was in much less danger now that the law-abiding paranormals saw him as an advocate, not a threat.

At that moment, Hank, Chris, Dan, and Remy walked over.

"This place is looking mighty pretty," Hank said, heading over to his wife and giving her a kiss on the cheek.

The white and gold decorations looked perfect in the spring weather. They gave the house and yard a festive air. The moon and stars motif also referenced the Harvest Moon theme Ana had planned for her October wedding, although the wolves were more likely to think of it as a Hunter's Moon. While the ceremony needed to be held at the full moon according to wolf tradition, this party was not being held when the moon was at its zenith because of the number of non-paras who would be in attendance. Ana had a lot of friends in the non-para world, and Sophie wanted to bring some of her school friends, also.

Hank and Ida didn't want to take the chance on anyone deciding to shift at an inopportune moment. Cassandra, the high priestess of the local coven, and some of her witches were arriving soon to cast protection and privacy spells around the farm. These would keep the non-para's from noticing any slips a paranormal might make as well as protecting the homestead from anyone attempting to come in and create a disturbance. Most of the leaders of the local paranormal groups would be here this evening. It would be a perfect time for someone with evil intent to cause havoc.

Living in secrecy and with these types of safeguards had always been just a way of life for the paranormals of Rivelou. They were lucky. Because of the location of their town at the nexus of several ley lines, and the years of work by people like Hank and the chief of police, for many years the paranormals of Rivelou had had much more freedom than those living in other areas. But they still knew to be careful.

"I think we're done here," Ida said as she began to gather up the scissors, extra confetti packages, and the other tools the women had used to decorate. "Shannon, you have your dress here to change into, don't you? I'd hate for you to have to drive all the way home and back again before the party starts."

"Yes, I've got everything in the car that I need. Including my gift for Ana and Chris. I'll go get it all now."

"And since you came with Ana and Chris, Dave Thorne can drive you home," Channing said suggestively. "He's really hot, you know, and he's needed someone to settle him down. I used to have a crush on him in high school."

Shannon's smile tightened at the thought of the beautiful shapeshifter having a crush on David although it was obvious from what she said that it was no longer the case. Shannon wondered who the mysterious man was that Channing was seeing. It was obvious to her that the girl was dating someone, but she'd been particularly closed mouth on that score.

CHAPTER 25

The party was in full swing when Dave arrived later that afternoon. There was a band playing under a big oak tree near the front of the house, children running in the yard, and several men, many of whom he knew, were drinking beer on the porch. He was greeted noisily by the group as he mounted the stairs.

"Hey, glad you could make it," Chris said, slapping him on the back. "Shannon's inside with the ladies."

"Yeah, you better go claim her," Dan said, holding out a beer. "A lot of guys already have their eyes on her."

"A growl came from Dave at the thought of other men sniffing around his woman. His woman? He only wished it were true. Then he hoped Chris hadn't noticed. He wasn't sure what Chris thought about his sister getting involved with someone new.

Obviously, Dan heard him though. "You're starting to sound like a real wolf instead of just a witch," he teased.

"I thought we were supposed to be on the down-low today," he said.

"Eh, no one around but us paras right now; besides Cassandra and your lot have used some incantations and spells for privacy and protection. We should be pretty safe from anyone who shouldn't notice anything."

"I wouldn't mind Ana's friend Monica noticing me," said Gabe, Dan's best friend since grade school. "Even if she is a non-para." Monica was a fellow admin with Ana in the history department at the University of Rivelou.

"Hey, I thought Ana told both of you to keep your hands off her best friend," Chris said.

"Little sisters can ask; big brothers don't always have to obey," Dan said with a laugh. He had noticed another friend of his sister's, Kathleen. He had no intention of heeding his sister's warning about this friend.

"And I'm only a friend of the brother," said Gabe. "I can

play by my own rules."

"You don't think Monica has any say in this?" David asked. "I've met her before, and trust me, she has a mind of her own."

"That's just means she's ready to be persuaded by me," Gabe bragged.

They all laughed, and Dave said, "I think I'm going to leave you boys to your fantasies, go find Shannon, and say hello to everyone inside." Dave headed into the house.

It didn't take him long to complete his quest and find Shannon. She was standing in the front room of the old farmhouse with Ana, Abby, and several other women. She was wearing a blue sundress that bared her shoulders enticingly. He walked up behind her, put an arm around her, and gave her a quick kiss on the cheek.

"Remember, this is part of your cover. Don't bite my head off; I have to kiss you," he whispered when he felt her stiffen. He was sure she had been about to turn around and give him hell Shannon-style. While he enjoyed riling her up sometimes, just for the fun of it, this was not the day. And besides, he'd wanted to kiss her, and the undercover job was a good excuse.

"Dave, I'm so glad you could make it." Ana held out her hand to him.

"Thanks so much for letting me crash the party with Shannon."

"Of course, we're happy to have you. Do you know many people here? I can introduce you around."

"Well, he certainly knows me," he heard a familiar voice and turned to see his aunt, Winnie's mother. He gave her a hug. "I should have known you'd be her, Aunt Lena."

"Your uncle is downstairs with Mr. Bertrand and some of the other men, and Winnie's around here someplace, also."

"Great. I'm glad she's getting out. Is she doing better?"

"I hope so," Lena said, with a worried look on her face.

"Oh, what's the matter with Winnie? She's such a sweetheart. I hope it's nothing serious," asked Ana.

"She was friends with one of the girls who was killed in the Artificial Witch Murders," Lena answered.

"Oh no. That's terrible. Dave, Shannon, do they have any new leads about who's doing it?"

"Nothing we can talk about," Shannon said quickly.

"I should really say hello to our hosts," Dave added, putting his arm back around Shannon's waist and moving them away from the group, effectively ending a conversation neither of them wanted to get into.

"Do we really have to put on the act today?" Shannon complained as she attempted to extract herself from Dave's arm.

"Maybe it's not an act to me," he said, pulling her closer. "I thought I should talk to Mr. Bertrand, by the way; I want you to come with me," he headed down the basement stairs.

They found Hank, his son Remy who was Ana's dad, Dave's Uncle Luke, and several other men sitting back and watching a baseball game on the big screen TV in the comfortable family room that took up most of the basement of the spacious old home.

He greeted everyone, gave his uncle a quick hug, then turned to Hank. "Nice of you to have me, Sir."

"I'm hearing good things about you from Chief Anderson.

"He's a good boss; I'm very happy working with him."

"Shannon, I'm hearing some good news about you, too." The older man turned to her.

Shannon rolled her eyes, and her mouth tightened in a frown.

"Oh, I know, girl; you don't want any shifters up in your business, but that's the way we are in the Bertrand pack, and you're just going to have to get used to it. Your brother is marrying my granddaughter, and that makes you and me family—and if there is one thing we shifters are good at, it's taking care of family." The other men raised their glasses and cans in agreement with Hank's words.

"And now you're thinking does 'family' mean he's got to butt his nose in where it isn't wanted?'" Hank continued. "Well, sometimes it does."

Shannon tried hard to keep the angry expression on her face, but she couldn't help laughing. "Hank, you're incorrigible. Everything Ana says about you is true."

"If she says I'm an interfering, meddling old man, she'd be right. Why don't you two sit down and have a beer with us? And no, we won't pump you for information on these murders."

"That's because you can get all the information you want from the chief," Shannon said teasingly. Dave was surprised. Hank Bertrand had managed to make Shannon more relaxed than he'd ever seen her.

They sat down with the men, and Dave asked about the game. It was the Cardinals versus the Royals, and everyone in the room had an opinion on who would win and why.

After a few minutes, though, Dave's uncle brought the conversation around to the coven. "Shannon, I hear Dave's giving you a refresher course on some of your spells and magic," he said.

Shannon actually smiled this time. "That's a really nice way to put it, Mr. Thorne," she said. "I was so rusty Dave's had to take me back to kindergarten—and I admit there are probably a lot of things I learned to do the wrong way, the first time around."

"We've heard a little about your upbringing—now don't worry, Dave hasn't been gossiping about you. But word gets around, and while your mother may have kept you away from the covens in Chicago, she was… well… known to many people both there and here."

Shannon blushed and turned her head. "I hadn't realized her reputation had spread beyond Chicago, but yes, now that you say it, I'm not surprised. Some of the things she did… well…."

"Have you heard anything from her since you left?" Luke said.

Something tightened inside of her. Why was he asking this question now? No one had mentioned her mother in years. Of course, she had made it her business to stay away from anyone who had known her mother. But now she began to wonder. Did David's uncle suspect something? Or was he just making conversation? She put on a blank face. "No, no sir. I haven't heard a word from her since the day Chris and I ran away from her house."

"I find that kind of unusual, don't you?"

"Well, we did make it our business not to be found."

"No one else has heard anything about her either," he continued.

"I really don't think you ever will."

CHAPTER 26

After the conversations with Hank and Dave's uncle Luke, Shannon was ready for some fresh air—and a drink. Dave seemed to understand that she'd had enough. He made their excuses, and they headed upstairs where they found the party in full swing. Dancing had begun in the barn so they headed over to watch, and before she could protest, Dave swung her out on the dance floor where they joined the crowd. The next hour or so was spent alternating between dancing and catching their breath.

Then the call came that dinner was being served. Dave nibbled her neck as they stood in line waiting for the food. "I'd like to eat you," he said. She blushed and giggled, then immediately felt guilty again. It was all part of the undercover act, she assured herself. She wasn't really enjoying Dave's flirting. Maybe telling herself that would make her feel less guilty.

At dinner she noticed Abby sitting with Jake Waseaux and started to head that way, but Dave steered her to a table with a group that included his aunt and uncle and cousin Winnie. Winnie was much more welcoming to Shannon than she had ever been before. She seemed to have forgiven Shannon for whatever she'd felt was wrong when they had first met. Maybe it was because Dave had staked a claim on her and she wasn't protesting. Well, she understood being protective of your family. She'd felt the same about Ana when Chris had first met her.

Sitting at the table was Cassandra, the high priestess of the local coven. Dave introduced her. She was a middle-aged woman who wore her snow-white hair long and straight, hanging to her waist. Except for a few laugh lines around her eyes, her face was unwrinkled. As head of the coven, Shannon had expected her to be dressed in a flowing caftan, but she wore jeans, a pretty pink blouse and gold, high-heeled sandals which showed off her pink pedicure.

"I hear that David is tutoring you," Cassandra said when

they were introduced.

"Yes, he's an excellent teacher.

"Yes he is; he is going to make a fine High Priest someday. You're going to have to come before the coven to be accepted, of course," Cassandra said. "But I'm hearing good things about you now, so it shouldn't be a problem. Particularly if you keep practicing your skills with David."

Shannon tried to pretend she wasn't surprised when she heard that Dave was considered High Priest material. She'd always thought of him as a fun-loving, motorcycle riding player. Yes, he took his job as a cop seriously, and he obviously cared deeply for his family, but this was a new side of him she hadn't known about. It made her admire him a little more.

"I understand you're going to want to talk to me, but I do feel I need a little more training first. There are so many things that I don't know."

"We know that your upbringing was—unusual," Cassandra paused as if trying to find the right word that would not insult Shannon. "But with David and Hank Bertrand vouching for you it shouldn't be any problem for you to join us. I think it would be better for you to have the support of your fellow witches as you learn new ways of using your power."

In other words, Shannon thought, you want to keep an eye on me. Well, she couldn't really blame them.

Shannon realized that Cassandra had continued speaking and quickly tuned back into the conversation.

"I do wish we knew where your mother was. Beatrix Spier was infamous. She hasn't been heard from in almost ten years. She has obviously gone to ground but that doesn't mean she can't stir up trouble again. Do you have any idea where she is?"

Shannon paled again. David noticed and took her hand gently. She liked the reassurance; she just wondered what he would think if he knew what had really happened to her mother.

Recovering from her surprise at her mother being brought into the conversation twice in one day, she answered, "I really couldn't tell you." It wasn't a lie. There was no way she would tell anyone where her mother was. Not even Chris knew. The only person she'd ever told was Jason.

The conversation moved on, and Shannon breathed a sigh of relief. Chris and Ana wandered over to greet everyone.

"Can I steal my sister for a few minutes?" he asked David. "I've hardly had a chance to see her lately."

They took a walk toward the cornfield which had been planted a few weeks before. Tiny, pale green sprouts could be seen peeking from the ground.

She hugged her brother close. "I'm so glad to see you this happy, Chris. For a while I never thought you were going to allow yourself to find someone to love. And you and Ana seem to fit so well together."

"You didn't think that at first, as I remember," Chris chuckled.

"Well, I wasn't the only one. And by the way, I'll have to tell you what I heard Ana's mother saying earlier."

Chris made a face. "Let's save Donna for another conversation. She can be a bit of a sour pickle. And I want to talk about you. I'm happy to see you with Dave."

"We aren't really together, you know."

"It sure looks like it from here. I think most of the people at this party think you two are together."

"It's just an act. It's not real. It's for an undercover assignment. I can't tell you any more about it."

"I've seen the way Dave looks at you. I don't think it's just an act as far as he's concerned. He's a good man, Shannon, and I think he really cares about you."

"I know. And I feel bad about it. But I just can't care for him. It wouldn't be right."

"Because of Jason?"

"Of course because of Jason. I can't ever have a relationship like that again. It would be betraying Jason's memory."

"You know he wouldn't want you to spend the rest of your life alone. He'd want you to have a new relationship. To fall in love again."

"I know, I know. I just feel like I'm betraying him every time I'm with David, Chris. The other day we…"

She stopped.

"You what?

"We had sex," she said reluctantly. "I can't believe I'm telling you this. I would think as my big brother you ought to go all old-school on him and threaten him if he hurts me."

Chris laughed. "If anyone needs protection, it's David. I think I need to threaten you and tell you not to hurt him."

"I already have. Like I said, we had a good time—a great time, actually. And when I woke up the next morning, I was so ashamed I just ran out of his house. I'm not sure why he's forgiven me for hurting him like that. I can't do it again. I figured it would be better to just cut things off before they got started, but now we have this assignment, and, well…"

"I never thought I'd be encouraging my little sister to go into a relationship with someone when she was reluctant, but in this case, yes, you should. Think about it, Shannon. You deserve to be happy. Jason would want it. You deserve another relationship and the chance of children. He wouldn't want you to lock yourself away emotionally for the rest of your life."

Shannon had tears in her eyes. "All right, all right. I'll try. I won't push David away anymore. And by the way, you do know you're a great big brother, right?"

"Yeah, I know it. I'm glad you do, too." He laughed and gave her a hug. They had come to the edge of the cornfield. They either needed to turn back or walk on into the woods that surrounded the farm.

"I'm going to go find Ana again. Are you ready to get back to the party, or do you need a few more minutes alone?"

"Alone, please. I need some time to think about what you said."

"I'll take that as a good sign that you plan to listen to your brother."

"Well, how about we compromise? I promise to think about what you said."

Chris laughed, gave her a hug, and headed back toward the party. Shannon watched him go, then continued her solitary walk under the trees.

CHAPTER 27

The shadows of dusk made it dark under the trees as Shannon walked on. The weather might be warm for spring, but the days were still short. She heard voices. Wasn't that Ana?

She was about to interrupt the conversation and say hello when she could tell by the tone of the voices that the discussion had become serious.

Now what did she do? She didn't want them to think that she was eavesdropping, so she just stayed where she was in the trees. And who was Ana speaking to? She listened more closely and recognized the other person as Ana's shapeshifter friend Connor.

"I can't help how I feel, Ana; it's not going to change."

"You've got to get over this, Connor. I care about you too much to let you ruin your life like this."

What were they talking about? Did it have anything to do with the Artificial Witch Murders? Was Connor somehow involved? Did he know something? What could he be up to that would ruin his life?

Shannon had met the man a few times, and he seemed nice enough. She knew he was a close friend of both Ana and her brother Dan, and an attorney, but that was all. She stayed out of sight at the edge of the trees. It would be too embarrassing to come out right now, and if she walked the other way, they would probably hear her. She didn't like eavesdropping, but if there was a chance Connor knew something about the murders... Her decision made, she stayed as quiet as she could, listening.

"I'm not ruining my life. I just want what you and Chris have. I'm not going to settle for anything less, so if I live my life alone, so be it. You settled when you married Jonathan Dugan and look how that worked out for you."

"It brought me Sophie. What could be a better result than that?"

"Well, that's the last thing I need."

Shannon felt herself blushing. She'd used her job as an excuse to eavesdrop, and now she was hearing a very personal conversation and wished she weren't. There was no way she was going to move now. She didn't want her future sister-in-law to think she was a little snoop.

"I just meant there are other things that a marriage could bring you besides marrying the love of your life," Ana continued.

"I've found her. She doesn't want me," he said bitterly. If I'd been a smarter man, I would have come to you a long time ago, when we were still in high school… or college… or when you finally saw the light and dumped Dugan. But I was too afraid you'd reject me."

"Oh, Connor. I've always loved you, just not like that. You're like a brother to me. You need to find someone else."

They moved on, and Shannon stood with her mouth open. So, Connor was in love with Ana. It was obvious she didn't return it. She wondered if Chris knew. No, probably not. There were some things you didn't share with anyone. Not even the love of your life. At least Ana's secret wasn't as black as Shannon's was.

Shannon walked back to the dancing where she noticed Ana's brother Dan flirting and dancing with Ana's best friend and coworker, Monica. Wow, for an engagement party that was supposed to bring people together, this one was turning into a bit of a shambles for Ana. First one friend confessed he loved her, and now her brother was flirting with her non-para best friend. Monica was the last person a shifter should get involved with. The woman lived to gossip. If things hadn't been bespelled so that the non-para's wouldn't notice anything unusual at this party, it would have been a disaster with Monica here. She watched as a shifter at the edge of the dance floor allowed a claw to appear on his hand and used it to flip off the top of a beer bottle.

She was shaking her head in disbelief at the carelessness when Abby and Ana came up to her.

What's that look for," Abby asked, throwing her arm around Shannon's shoulders. "You should be out dancing with that hunk of a partner of yours, not standing here in the shadows making faces."

"I was just noticing the shifter over there—I don't know

his name—pull out his claw just to open a beer bottle. I know Cassandra and the rest of the coven bespelled the party, but really, don't you think a little discretion is in order?"

"Oh, don't worry so much, Shannon. You're always so serious. This is a party. Relax. And we want to tell you how great it is to see you together with David." Abby nodded to Ana.

"Yes, Honey. I'm so glad to see you finally with someone. It makes me so happy to know you're finding what I've found with your brother," Ana added.

"Guys, I'm not sure it's like that. I don't know if I can ever really open myself up to someone after Jason."

"Shannon, I'm sure he was a wonderful man, but I know he wouldn't want you to spend the rest of your life mourning him. You're much too young for that."

"That's exactly what my brother said, Ana. You must have been talking with him."

"No, I swear. This is all Abby and me. We want you to be happy, and you look happy when you're with Dave."

"And you're good for him, too, Honey. He seems much more settled and responsible in the last few weeks. People are already starting to notice," added Abby. "You heard what Cassandra said when we were eating about him becoming a High Priest someday, didn't you?"

"So, I should be with Dave because I make him a better person?"

"No! Absolutely not. That's not what I meant, and you know it. You should be with Dave because he makes you happy. We can all see the difference in you."

"What if I told you it was all an act? That we're just doing this for an undercover assignment."

There, she'd just done what everyone on the force had told her not to do; she'd confessed that she and David were working an undercover assignment. She took a deep breath. "Please, forget I said that," she said, turning to both of her friends. "I shouldn't have said anything, but everyone is telling me how great Dave is, and how I should just forget Jason and…"

"No one is telling you to forget Jason. We're just saying that you don't need to spend the rest of your life alone just because he died," said Ana.

"And this may be just an undercover assignment for you, but for Dave, it's very real. You can't fake the smile he gets on his face every time he looks at you. I've known him a long time; I've seen him with other women, but he's different with you. He's happier, more relaxed. He's in love with you, Shannon, even if he hasn't admitted it yet."

"And it isn't all one-sided, either, Shannon, if you'd only admit it. Abby and I haven't known you very long, but we also see how you look at him."

"So, okay, I do lust after him, a little." She blushed." But that's all it is. I'm scratching an itch, and I feel guilty enough about that without worrying about love."

"Honey, Chris has told me about Jason. He was a wonderful man, I know, but from everything I've learned he'd be happy for you."

"Again, that's exactly what Chris says."

"Well, I know it's hard when a big brother is right, but maybe this one time you should listen to him."

Shannon nodded. Maybe they were right. Maybe it was time she finally buried her feelings for Jason and started living again.

CHAPTER 28

At that moment Ana was distracted from the conversation as she noticed her sister heading out to the dance floor hand-in-hand with a handsome, dark-haired man. "Oh my God! What the hell is Channing thinking bringing him here?" She started to head toward the pair when Abby stopped her with a hand on her arm.

"Ana, don't. You don't know what's going on. It could all be innocent, and you don't want to call any more attention to them than you have to."

Ana stopped. "You're right, but I don't see how they could have made themselves more obvious than they already have."

"What are you two talking about? What's wrong?" Shannon asked.

"My sister. The idiot. Do you see who she's dancing with?"

"He's very nice-looking," Shannon ventured. The man, who looked to be in his late thirties, wore the jeans and t-shirt that many of the men at the party sported. The outfit flattered him way more than it did most of the men there even though many were werewolves and certainly in good shape, Shannon thought as she looked the unknown man over. The muscles of his arms strained the seams of his shirt, and it stretched over his torso in a way that hinted at a very impressive six-pack. She noticed how his jeans hugged his thighs, not to mention his butt, when he twirled Channing around on the dance floor.

"Damn! He's hot," she said.

"He's not just hot, he's an explosion waiting to happen," said Ana.

"Why? What's the matter? I mean, yeah, he looks like he's a little older than Channing—she's what, 25 right? But they're only dancing."

"His name is Dolan McTier. His father is Michael McTier, the Alpha of the McTier Clan, on the Ohio River near

Lexington. They've been trying to take over our pack for years."

"And you invited him to your engagement party?" Shannon asked, surprised the man was here considering Ana's reaction.

"No, I did not invite him here. Obviously, he came with Channing. I told her, of course, that she could bring a date; it just never, never occurred to me that it would be Dolan McTier. I didn't even know she knew him."

Shannon looked around and noticed that the crowd was growing quiet as one by one people noticed the pair dancing in the center of the barn. Several of the other dancing couples backed away, and pretty soon the two were alone on the floor.

At that moment, Tyler and Winnie walked into the barn and up to Ana, Shannon, and Abby. "Hey guys, what's the deal?" asked Tyler. "Everyone's awful quiet. We were going to dance."

Abby just pointed at the pair in the middle of the floor.

"What the hell!" Tyler said. He turned and ran out of the barn, leaving Winnie standing with her mouth open in surprise.

"Damn it, he's gone to get Dan," said Abby. "What can we do to head this off? Ana, where's Chris?"

"He was getting us some drinks and was going to come right here, but he must have stopped to talk to someone."

"I'll go get him—and Dave, too, if I see him," said Shannon, and she quickly followed Tyler out of the barn.

It didn't take her long to spot her brother, Dave, and several other men, including Hank and Ana's father Remy, talking in a group under the oak tree. Chris had two beers in his hand. Obviously, he'd been heading to Ana when he'd been waylaid by his friends.

"Chris, Ana needs you," she said.

A couple of the men started to make a joke about his fiancée needing him, but Chris stopped them with a hand motion as he noticed the seriousness of Shannon's expression. "What's wrong?"

"I'm not really sure. Channing is dancing with a man named Dolan McTier and..."

"What the fuck?"

"The damn bastard!"

"I'll show him not to trespass on our land and take advantage of my daughter!"

The comments flew thick and fast even as the men took off toward the barn at a run. Shannon stared in surprise for a moment before rushing after them.

When she got back, she had to push her way through the crowd that had formed. She finally reached Abby, Ana, and Winnie. Monica and Kathleen were now standing with them. Monica, for once was not saying anything as she watched, mouth open, as Dan confronted Channing and Dolan McTier. Tyler stood right behind him, his posture shouting that he was ready to back his brother up at any moment.

"What is the matter, Danny? You're being ridiculous. I'm just dancing," Channing said.

"Dancing with him." Dan thrust his chin toward Dolan, who took a step toward him.

"And since when is dancing a crime against pack rules? I…"

At that moment Chris, Dave, and the other men pushed their way into the center of the crowd.

"It's a problem when you're dancing with my daughter," said Remy. Shannon was astonished. Ana and Channing's father was quiet, scholarly. She'd never seen him like this; he seemed to have grown larger, his expression feral as he snarled his anger at the interloper. His sudden transformation was a revelation to her as she suddenly understood, in a way she never had before, the power of an Alpha werewolf. He bared his teeth and growled at Dolan.

Ana turned to Abby. "Get Monica out of here and—there, Jake can help you," she said as the man came up next to them.

"Abby, she can't remember any of this. And Jake, can you get some of your coven to make sure the non-para's are safe and unaware? We need to head this disaster off before it becomes any worse."

"I'll get Cassandra. We can suggest to the non-para's that the party's over; start them on their way home."

"Good, good," Ana said, her attention divided between Jake and what was happening on the dance floor.

Channing had stepped in front of Dolan even as Dan pushed his father to the side so he was at the front of his own pack of wolves.

Wow, Channing had a lot of guts, Shannon thought, watching the scene play out. Stepping between a bunch of Alpha males, even if you are a werewolf yourself, was either really courageous or really stupid. Maybe a little of both.

"Danny, you are being ridiculous. I told you, I'm just having a dance with Dolan. It's not like I'm…"

Dan cut her off with a growl. "You should know better than to dance with someone like him."

Chris now stepped up and tried to reason with everyone. Fat lot of good that was going to do, Shannon scoffed to herself.

"Everyone needs to calm down. This is no place…"

But his words had no effect. Dan and Dolan growled at each other and began to change. They both pulled off their shirts and stripped out of their jeans even as their claws and fangs appeared, the shape of their faces sharpening. The non-para's in the crowd were going to get an eyeful of naked man, even if it only took a few seconds before they changed and two wolves were standing in the middle of the dance floor.

Shannon looked around frantically. The paranormals were pushing in to get a better view. At the same time, most of the people that she was sure were non-para's were heading out of the barn, chatting with each other happily, oblivious to everything going on around them. It looked odd, the two groups so obviously different group, but thank the goddess!

She'd never seen witchcraft used in this manner. It was awe-inspiring. She looked back at the center of the barn and realized David was no longer with the group of mostly werewolves confronting Dolan. He'd probably gone to help Cassandra with the spells. She wished she could help, too, but she didn't have enough knowledge yet to do so. It was a goal.

Turning her attention back to the center of the barn, Dan and Dolan had completed the change to wolf and were circling each other. Her attention had been drawn away just as the change took place, and she wasn't sure now which wolf was Dan and which Dolan. One of them was a grey and white coloration, the other more reddish brown. They feinted, attacking each other simultaneously. Fur flew as each wolf attempted to take a bite out of the other. The fight had just begun to get serious. The grey wolf a grip on the back of the red wolf's neck and threw him across the room. The red wolf jumped up, snarling, and circled the other slowly, looking for an advantage.

Suddenly, Chief Anderson arrived at the edge of the circle of onlookers.

"Enough!" he shouted, lifting his hands in the air.

The two wolves stopped in their tracks. "Change—now! And get yourselves decent."

The pair became human again faster than Shannon thought possible. They quickly picked up the clothes that they had discarded and pulled on their jeans.

"All right, the show's over," the chief said. He had lowered his hands, and his voice no longer held the commanding air of the siren, but he was still impressive.

Hank Bertrand joined him. "All right, folks, let's get back to celebrating Ana's and Chris's engagement. I believe there is cake and coffee outside for anyone who wants dessert, and our band is ready to start up again if anyone is still interested in dancing."

The crowd slowly moved along, some heading outside, others starting to dance again as the band began to play Neil Young's "Harvest Moon."

Dave came up behind her just then and put his arms around her. "Can I steal a beautiful woman away for a dance?"

CHAPTER 29

Shannon relaxed into Dave's embrace. Yes, she wanted another dance with him. She wanted to dance all night. She wanted to quit being a widow and be young again.

"Yes," she said, putting her arms around his neck. "I'm ready." Dave smiled, understanding her answer was about more than just a dance.

They stayed in the barn, swaying together until the party was over and the band was putting away their instruments.

"Take a ride with me tonight?" Dave asked. "I came on my motorcycle."

"Yes. I rode out with Ana. My car's not here, so I don't have to worry about it."

They drove through the night, enjoying the breeze in their hair and the smell of spring. And somehow they ended up at Dave's house. David kissed her as he helped her off the bike. "You taste so good." He pulled her closer to him.

She responded by deepening the kiss. Her arms reached under his leather jacket, pulling up his t-shirt to stroke the hard muscles of his back. It felt wonderful to touch him, to not worry about anything but what she felt right now, in this moment.

"Are you sure about this? I can wait, you know. Maybe like last time we should have a witchcraft lesson before we even think about anything more." He was a fool, he knew, for suggesting they wait. But he didn't want her to regret anything. He couldn't help that his arms tightened around her, moving their hips together so she could feel just how much he wanted her.

Shannon appreciated his willingness to wait; she knew he was sincere, even as his body betrayed his words. For her, he would forego his own needs, take it as slowly as she needed. But the time for that was past. She wanted this man. She had finally admitted it to herself, and if she didn't act now she would just begin to have doubts again. That would do neither of them any good.

"No, I think witchcraft is like driving; you shouldn't do it when you've been drinking. We should just try something different tonight," she said with a giggle.

"But what about driving here on the motorcycle?"

"You weren't drinking; you quit over an hour ago. I noticed."

"So you've been watching me," he said with a satisfied smile.

"Yes. I always watch you when you aren't looking," she admitted.

His grin got even wider as he did a mental fist pump. She'd been watching him. She had wanted him even when she wouldn't admit it. "Okay, then, my bedroom it is."

They moved toward the house and up the porch stairs, kissing and touching, teasing each other as they went. Once they made it inside, David kicked the front door shut, then picked her up and carried her into his bedroom.

It was dark tonight; there was no moon. Only the light from a few stars relieved the blackness of the room. David kissed her again, and Shannon caught her breath in anticipation as he flicked his wrist, lighting the candles that sat on the dresser. They flickered as if stirred by an unseen breeze, their flames bending toward each other just as David bent toward her, ready to kiss her once again.

He set her down at the edge of the bed, her breathing unsteady. David's fingertips grazed the inside of her wrist, then moved slowly up her arm, light as a charm whispered at midnight. The touch sent a ripple through her like a spell too long uncast, stirring power buried deep beneath the guilt that still tried to pull at her, despite her brother's and her friends' advice, despite her own brave words.

Could she do this? She'd just told David yes, but she still wasn't sure. She tried to pull her hand back, but he held her gently, his thumb tracing lazy circles on her skin, the soft sensation ramping up the anticipation of his hands touching her in other places.

"You still don't have to do this," David said, his voice low, rough as incense smoke. "I can feel your hesitation. Don't do this just for me. You don't owe me anything. We can quit now, and I'll take you home." It might kill him to do that, he thought, but he would if that were what she needed.

"I know you would, but you don't have to," she whispered; the truth knotted behind her ribs even as she said yes. She knew she didn't owe David, but what did she owe Jason?

The name twisted in her mind like an incantation gone awry, a memory she couldn't banish. Guilt slithered over her skin. She shut her eyes tight, but that only made it worse—the ghost of Jason's hands against her body, his laugh in her ear. She felt like a traitor just sitting here, her heart tangled between past and present. But she needed to do this. She needed to banish Jason's ghost if she were ever going to move on.

David cupped her cheek, drawing her back into the present. His dark eyes glimmered with understanding, not pity. She'd forgotten what it was like to be seen so clearly; no one ever had but Jason. And as she thought that, her husband's ghost receded farther from her mind.

"It's just us here," he told her, his breath warm against her lips. "No one else, and nothing else matters. Not tonight."

Magic hummed between them in a low, steady pulse, like the earth breathing beneath their feet, the flowers coming to life in the warm, spring night air. Shannon felt it thrum along her spine, pooling under her skin where his hand pressed against her side. It was dangerous to get this close to someone again, but it was also dangerous to deny what was inside of her.

"I don't know if I can..." Her voice cracked as she admitted the truth, and she lowered her eyes from his and stared down at the floor, ashamed.

David slid his hand slowly back down her arm. It was as if his fingertips grazed the scars she always kept hidden, the traces of the evil spells her mother had forced her to cast. His touch banished all other thoughts, even the last remnants of the love she'd lost when Jason died. Though those scars were bittersweet, and she didn't want to let them go, she knew she must or she would never be whole again.

David seemed to sense what she was thinking. He didn't ask a question; he didn't say a word. He just kissed the path his fingers traced; each touch as deliberate as a sigil drawn with care.

"You're allowed to want this," he whispered against her skin. "You're allowed to feel alive. I didn't understand before what it would mean to you to be intimate with another man— with me. I pushed you too hard. Maybe you're making me grow up." He grinned at her. "You didn't think that was possible, did you? But I'm thinking about more than just what I want this time. I want you. But I want you to want me even more. I want you to be at peace with your decision. I want you to be ready for a new relationship when you come to me. And I'm willing to wait if that's what you need."

His words were like an enchantment undoing the knot tied too tightly inside her for so long. Slowly, she let herself lean into him, her body softening like wax warmed by a flame. The tension between them thickened; electric, it was both new and old, a ritual performed countless times but never quite the same, with an old love or with a new.

David's lips found hers—soft, patient, as if coaxing a spell to life. Shannon kissed him back tentatively at first, but soon it deepened again, a spark igniting. The guilt was still there, a shadow lingering at the edges, but it didn't own her. Not anymore.

His hands moved over her body, awakening her like the spring coaxing the first buds into bloom. Every touch left her skin buzzing with energy, magic simmering beneath her flesh. She pressed closer, seeking the warmth of his body, the steadiness of his breath.

He slowly pulled off his jacket, then his t-shirt. His skin glowed beneath her fingertips as his tattoos flared to life.

He whispered her name, and it felt like a sacred word, spoken only for her. "You see what you do to me. You set my power on fire," he said. She felt herself slipping, surrendering, the walls around her heart crumbling like old parchment in a fire.

David slowly tugged her own shirt out from her jeans. Her skin felt so smooth beneath his palms. They sat touching each other, learning each other. She traced patterns along his chest, following the lines of his tattoos. He grazed her breast with his hand, and she moaned. Yes, it felt good. It felt right. She wanted more. He cupped her breast more tightly, teasing her nipples until she moaned. Never before had she dared to invoke this kind of magic. Never used these spells with Jason. David's tattoos flared ever more brightly as her fingers traced teasingly over his body. He groaned softly, the sound vibrating through her, and for the first time in what felt like forever, she laughed.

He murmured something—a fragment of an incantation—and the air shimmered with energy. Their power wove together, threads of gold—that was David—and silver— that was her— twining like lovers. The magic danced along their skin, warming and sparking with each touch.

They tumbled down to lie on the bed, tasting, touching, their breath mingling. The guilt whispered again at the edges of her mind, but David's voice was louder, his presence more real. He was here. Jason never would be again.

She banished the guilt—forever this time as finally Dave drew her legs apart, then hovered over her as if silently asking one more time if she were sure.

He caressed her breasts again, then bent to her nipples, taking first one, then the other into his mouth. She was ready to fly with the sensation. She couldn't stand it anymore. It was too much and not enough.

"Please," she whispered. She wanted him inside her. He released her breast. Yes! She was so ready for him to take her. But instead he bent lower, lower, finally taking her in his mouth again. Oh yes, this was flying! She writhed under him, her hips moving back and forth until she could stand it no longer. She came apart, separating into a million, shimmering pieces of light, and finally coming back together again to stare up at him. His mischievous grin told her how much he had enjoyed making her come.

"Now it's my turn to do that to you," she said.

"No."

"No?"

"It's our turn to do that to each other."

When he entered her, it was like the final seal on the spell—a shift, a release, the thaw after a long winter. Magic surged between them, fierce and bright, filling the room.

Shannon gasped, arching beneath him, the sensation too big, too much, and exactly what she needed.

She matched his rhythm, back and forth, and with each thrust she felt herself returning to life; she felt her power returning. She had renounced magic not just for herself, but for Jason, and now it was time to take back all that she was. She was still here, still whole, still able to love. Her powers did not have to be a tool of destruction. It could create, just as she was creating something new and precious between herself and David.

As they moved together, David's gaze never left hers. His touch was an anchor, grounding her even as she unraveled, screaming his name, just as he called out hers. And as the magic crested and broke over them both, Shannon knew she'd finally made her peace. Jason was gone, but she was still here. Still living. Still loving.

The candles flickered, their flames rising high, as if in celebration.

CHAPTER 30

The next morning Dave woke up and reached over to the other side of the bed hoping to find a warm, soft body next to him. He planned to make love to Shannon in the glow of the morning light. To cuddle her, to treat her tenderly. To show her just how much she meant to him.

The bedcovers next to him were cold. Damn it. Had she run again? How could he show her what she meant to him? Particularly if she kept running away each time he got close. He ran his hand across his beard in frustration, then suddenly relaxed and sniffed the air. The scent of bacon and coffee wafted into the bedroom from the kitchen, and he could hear someone rattling around out there.

He smiled. She was making him breakfast. If that weren't a sign that she had accepted him as her lover, he didn't know what was. He got up and pulled on his jeans, not bothering to look for a shirt, and headed out to the kitchen. Shannon stood at the stove wearing only one of his flannel shirts. She must have found it in his closet. There was nothing to turn a man on more, he thought, than a woman dressed in his shirt—and nothing else. The garment skimmed just past her hips, showing off her legs prettily. He rose to the occasion and walked quietly over to hug her from behind, giving her a soft kiss on the neck.

"Oh! You startled me!" she said, whipping around, the spatula still in her hand, and giving him a quick smack on the shoulder. But he could tell from her smile she wasn't really upset.

"And who did you think would be kissing you in my kitchen if it weren't me?" he asked playfully.

"I wasn't thinking. I was daydreaming, I guess." She ran her hands over his bare chest with a murmured "mmh" of appreciation. It turned him on even more; he pressed her closer to him, making sure she could feel just how much he wanted her.

"Were you thinking about us? About another round in the bedroom this morning?" he asked hopefully.

"Well, that would be nice, but that's not actually where my mind was."

He gave her a silly pout, and she laughed before continuing. "I was thinking about some of the spells you taught me in the last week. Going over them in my mind, you know. I guess I'm ready to accept my powers and learn to use them the right way," she said.

"That's great. What brought about this change?" he asked. He headed over to pull the silverware out of the drawer as Shannon plated the eggs and bacon and poured the coffee.

When they sat down at his kitchen table, she answered him. "It was you. Last night. What we shared was magical. It got me thinking that it was something more than I'd ever shared with Jason. With him, I locked away all my magic. I'm not saying it wasn't good between us; it was. He was my first love, and I would have happily stayed with him forever if Jason were still..." She started to tear up.

"I know, Honey. I understand. You don't have to compare me to Jason. We are different, and what you had with him was different from what you can have with me. It's alright for you to miss Jason. I'll never make you feel as if you can't talk about him.

"But I do understand what you're saying. I've had sex with more than one woman; some had powers, some not. And when we both have power, the experience is just at a whole other level. But I still don't want you to think that what we shared last night was just because we're both witches. Yes, that was part of it, and it was also much more. There's something between us that is greater than I've ever shared with anyone else." He took a deep breath. Time to put his cards on the table. "I love you, Shannon. That's the difference."

Shannon started to get up from the table. "Don't say that. It's too soon. You can't know..."

He put a hand over hers, stopping her. "It's not. It's not too soon at all. I've loved you for quite a while now. I was attracted to you from the first moment I met you, but as I've gotten to know you these past few months as your partner, it's grown into something more.

"I love your prickly nature. I love the way you push back at me when you think I've gone too far. I love the way you stand up for what is right. I love your loyalty to Jason and to your brother—in fact to all of your friends. You fight for justice, Shannon, and I love that side of you just as much as the sexy way you look when you're angry at me, or the way you sympathize and want to help people who are the victims of a crime. I love all of you, don't you understand? You don't have to say the words back to me right now. I know you don't feel the same about me yet." He turned her hand over in his, clasping their fingers together, then brought it up to his lips for a quick kiss.

"I just hope that someday you will. I'm going to wait for you, Shannon. You take as long as you need. I'll be here." He stood up, still holding her hand. "But for right now, let's just have another witchcraft lesson. I want you to be as prepared as possible when you go to this 'empowerment meeting' on Wednesday. We don't know what you're going to find, and having a little bit of power at your fingertips should help matters."

"Okay, I can do that."

They cleaned up the breakfast dishes and adjourned to Dave's workroom. "I want to try you with some defensive spells this time," he explained. "Think about it like sparring. I'm going to attempt to attack you, and you're going to disarm me."

"I don't want to hurt you."

"We've got protections set up, remember? You won't be able to hurt me," he said, pointing to the large circle of salt that they stood inside, with the candles at the four cardinal points.

"Now the problem with most of these spells is they work best if you have some herbs, candles, a protection circle. In other words, all the things you aren't going to have with you when you are at this meeting."

"So what's the point if I don't have everything I need to work the spell?"

The point is to get so good, so fast at casting the spell, that you don't need all of the other things. All you need is your power, and it's enough."

Shannon nodded slowly.

"But that doesn't mean that I'm going to let you go in without any protection at all—just like I wouldn't let you try to take down an armed robber without a gun. There are charms you can wear that will help to give you protection."

He went to his cabinet and got out several herbs. "St. John's Wort, to ward off negative energy and promote mental clarity," he explained as he laid some packets of the dried leaves on the table. "Angelica root for shielding, and mugwort to help prevent injury and deflect psychic attacks."

Shannon watched silently but intently as he lit the four colored candles at the cardinal points of their protection circle. He raised his hands over the herbs on the table, and she could feel his power rise as he began to recite the spell.

"Herbs of light and power three,
Protect this witch from all who'd see
Her injured, or defenseless be.
St. John's Wort, guard and keep her free
From confusion—give her clarity.
Mugwort, keep her strong, and heal
Any injuries that might be revealed.
Angelica root protection bring
From harm by any living thing.
Cast out shadows, bring her light.
Keep her safe throughout the night.
As I will, so mote it be."

He lowered his arms and began to gather the herbs into a small cloth medicine bag that he had also put on the table. He slipped an amethyst bead on the cord, then knotted it around the bag, and slipped it over her head.

"I want you to wear this at all times."

Shannon wrinkled her nose. "It smells, Dave. People are going to think I'm wearing some weird and awful perfume."

"The smell will fade pretty quickly, and we don't know when or where an attack might come. Please, Shannon. I'll feel much more comfortable about you going to this meeting if you're wearing this."

"But we don't even think Salvia has any power, so why do I need to wear it?"

"The charm will protect you from more than just magical attacks; it can help with the physical, also. Please Shannon, keep it on. For me."

She held up the bag, still hanging around her neck, looked at it closely, sniffed it again, then tucked it under her shirt. "Okay, does that make you happy?"

He kissed her lightly on the nose. "Yes, it does. You're precious to me, and I want to know you're safe at all times."

CHAPTER 31

"This is great, but I thought we were going to work on teaching me something a little more active," Shannon said.

"Ah, there's my prickly Shannon, always questioning everything."

"I am not prickly!"

Dave just laughed at her.

"You promised some magical version of sparring," she said, bouncing on her toes and raising her fists. "The charm is awesome, but you did that. I need something I can actively do."

"Okay, then let's try a binding spell."

"What's that?"

"Exactly what it sounds like. It binds a person just as effectively, but a lot more quickly, than tying them up with a rope or handcuffing them. When done well it can literally stop someone in their tracks."

"That's sounds useful. I can think of a lot of perps I'd like to use it on."

"Yeah, I know what you mean, but remember, in our job we are not allowed to use spells on non-paras."

Shannon sighed, then grinned at him. "Yeah, I know. But I can dream, can't I? You know, when it's a Friday night, and we're breaking up a bar fight?"

"Yeah, I hear you," said Dave. "I've been tempted a few times." He laughed and added, "Okay, enough of that. Let's get back on track. Stand over there." He pointed to the other side of the wide circle of salt on the floor.

"Now come at me like you're going to attack," he said.

"You're sure."

"Trust me, Shannon, you're not going to hurt me."

"Okay," she said hesitantly, but she raised her fists, took a deep breath, and lunged toward him.

And stopped.

Her hands were still in the air, her left foot in front as if she were about to run.

"I can't move. I'm frozen. Dave!" She didn't know if she were more afraid, excited, or turned on.

Dave just grinned. He made a hand motion, and she was released from the spell so quickly she almost fell.

Dave rushed over to help her regain her balance, and she took the time to kiss him slowly.

"Ah, ah, ah. You are not going to distract me that way," he told her. Now I need to teach you how to do it to me. Here are the words to the incantation. You can repeat them after me.

"Bound and knotted by root and vine
Your limbs are still; your will is mine.
Frozen tight, you cannot flee,
Bound in place, so mote it be."

He repeated the incantation several times as he showed her how to push her magic toward him, using only a quick hand gesture. They worked for several minutes until she felt confident.

"Now, try this on me," Dave said.

"You're sure?"

"Yep, you aren't going to injure me, just stop me." He suddenly brought his hands up as if he were going to strike her, and with a motion so quick she almost didn't see it, Shannon froze him in place.

"That's great, Shannon. Now release me."

"I'm not sure I want to do that," she said teasingly. "I could just have my way with you right here, and you couldn't do a thing."

She approached him slowly, her hands wandering down his bare chest where his tattoos had once again begun to glow, showing her just how much he was enjoying her attention. Neither one of them had changed; he was still in only his jeans while she wore just his flannel shirt. Her hands continued to wander over his body, exciting him even more. She wandered lower, touching his hard cock through his jeans, rubbing up and down.

Dave groaned. "You're killing me here, Shannon. Release me. Please."

She rubbed him again and pulled down his zipper. "Are

you sure you want me to stop?"

He closed his eyes. He could break her spell any time he liked. She knew that, too, he was sure. But right now he wanted to see just what she was going to do. This was a new side of Shannon. She was relaxed and happy and playful, and so much more sensual than he'd ever seen her before.

"By the goddess, what you do to me," he groaned as she released his cock from his pants, slowly stroking him up and down.

She knelt in front of him and took him in her mouth. He caught his breath, then groaned again. He wanted to break this spell she had cast, hold her in his arms, and take her up against the wall. Right now. But she was testing her power, finding out exactly what she could do. And not just with her magic. She was testing her power as a woman, as his lover. He didn't want to deny her that. And besides, this felt... so... good...

He groaned again and let her have her way. It was magical. The flames on the candles, still lit around their circle, grew higher and higher until he couldn't hold back any longer. He shouted her name as he came in her mouth.

Shannon looked up at him and smiled. "I never knew doing magic could be such a turn-on," she said. She made the hand gesture he had shown her and released him from the binding spell so unexpectedly he almost fell over.

He steadied himself, then raised her from the floor. "Shannon, you are the most wonderful, sexy thing I've ever seen. He kissed her soundly. "But you're the one who said you wanted to practice defensive spells. You bound me; now, I think it's my turn to play strict teacher," he told her as he tucked himself back into his jeans.

"Ooo, are you going to punish me?"

"You sound much too excited about that idea for it really to be a punishment." It was difficult to force his mind away from scooping her up, taking her back to his bedroom, and doing every naughty she could think of to make her scream and beg for more. But he couldn't. She was going undercover at this meeting in just three days, and he wanted her to have every advantage possible. And that meant more practice.

"We've learned some things. I've got my new protection charm." She pulled the bag out of her shirt and showed it to him. "And I've learned this binding spell. Isn't that enough for one morning?"

"No. It is a lot, and you've done great, today, little witch, but the best defense is a good offense. There are a few more very valuable spells I want you to have in your armory. You may have heard of a few of them. The most important is *Incantare Thanatos.*"

CHAPTER 32

Shannon drew back from him with a hiss of anger. "You told me you didn't do black magic. You assured me your coven did nothing like that." She turned away from him and stomped out of the room. He stood for a moment in stunned surprise, then went after her and found her in his bedroom, digging through the sheets and comforter that had spilled on the floor as they made love. She began to pull on her clothes as soon as she found them.

"What's wrong, Shannon?"

"You're all the same, aren't you? Witches." The name was a curse when she said it. "I should have never let you drag me back. I'm out of here, David. I'm done. I'm sorry I can't help Captain Anderson find out who the Artificial Witch Murder culprit is, but I'm done. I'm finished. I'm finished with the police, I'm finished with Rivelou, and I'm finished with you."

She had found the rest of her clothing and put it on as she spoke. Now she turned to pick up her purse. Dave knew as soon as she had it in her hands she would be out the door, and he'd never see her again. He couldn't let that happen. He did something he would have sworn an hour before that he would never do to any innocent person, particularly not to Shannon. With a quick gesture of his hand and a few muttered words he froze her in place.

As she realized what he had done, she tried to struggle, tried to break free of the spell that bound her. But his power was strong, and she was still only his apprentice. The trick he had shown her earlier to release the binding spell wasn't going to work against his faster and more powerful magical abilities.

"Let. Me. Go. Now!" she said, her voice low and menacing.

"I will once you tell me what is wrong. I mention one spell, and you try to fly out of here so fast I thought you really did have a broomstick."

"You know what is wrong. You lure me back to

practicing magic with 'Oh, my coven is different; we only practice white magic.' Then the first chance you get you bring up *Incantare Thanatos*. There, I've explained it. Now let me go."

"You've explained nothing, Shannon. What is it about *Incantare Thanatos* that has you so freaked out?"

"It's black magic! That's what."

"It is not black! It does not do any permanent harm to the person." He ran his hand through his hair and down his beard as he always did when frustrated. "Okay, I can see where someone could use it for dark purposes, but that goes for just about any spell you can name. It's the intent that makes most of the spells we use white or black, not the spell itself."

Shannon rolled her eyes. It seemed to be the only part of her body she could move. "That sounds like a great way to rationalize anything you do. 'Oh, I meant it for good, so it can't really be bad.' But some things just *are* bad—they're wicked. Evil. And if that's what you practice, I don't want anything to do with it. Now would you let me go?"

"Not until you promise me you won't run from me, Shannon. That you won't just leave and not listen to what I have to say."

"All right. I promise."

"I'm not sure I believe you," he said, his cocky grin back in full evidence. "Just know I can and will stop you again if you try to leave." He made a gesture, and she was suddenly free of her bonds. Her arms fell down at her side in relief.

"Okay," she said. "I'm still here. I'm not running. Just say what you have to say."

"Yes, there are some things—some *spells*—that are inherently evil. But there are others that, depending on how they are used, can be either evil or good. It's not the spell; it's the intent."

"Hmph!"

David tried without success not to smile again as she crossed her arms over her chest and began tapping her toe. She was so cute when she was angry, but this was so not the time. He wiped the grin off his face as quickly as it had appeared. She knew more black magic and dark spells than he did or ever would, and he didn't want to tempt her.

"Let me give you an example. We joked earlier about using the binding spell on drunks at a bar brawl. Let's take it a step further. Let's say you've been called to a home because a husband and wife are fighting. You've been on calls like this. You know it happens in the paranormal community as much as it does with the N.P.'s."

Shannon nodded her head reluctantly.

"The male is strong. Way strong. Let's make him a bear shifter. And he's got hold of the wife, and he won't see reason, and you know that unless you act immediately, he's going to kill her. Then you use *Incantare Thanatos*. The male drops unconscious until you can get him in handcuffs. Then you release him from the spell."

Shannon opened her mouth to speak.

"But wait!" He lifted his hand in a stopping gesture. "There's one more thing I want you to know before you make up your mind. If you use this spell you will go up in front of a review board. If you're acting as a cop, the board will consist of other cops. If not, then the board will be only people from your own coven. We have laws here in Rivelou, Shannon, and we take them seriously. You can't just use dangerous spells for no good reason. But it is still to your advantage to know them—and to know the countermeasures in case someone uses them against you."

Shannon dropped onto the edge of his bed, her purse hung by its strap between her hands, her head sagged between her shoulders. Dave wanted to hold her, just hold her and comfort her until all of her fears and worries melted away. He knew she wasn't ready for that, though, wasn't ready for him. It hurt, but he accepted it. Whatever this anger about a spell was, he knew it wasn't really about him. It was rooted in her past.

"Shannon, tell me what happened to you that made you so upset when I mentioned this spell." He crouched down in front of her.

"I can't tell you."

"Can't or won't, Shannon? Don't you know I'm here for you? I'm not going to judge you, no matter what you say."

"I've never told anyone, David. Not anyone but Jason,

that is."

David tried to stem the rising jealousy that hit him like a tsunami. What could Shannon tell Jason, a non-para, about magic that she couldn't discuss with him? He wanted to get angry and force her to tell him, to let her know that she had to let him in on her secret if she trusted him. But that wasn't the right way to handle this. He knew it, and as hard as it was, he took a deep breath and forced the anger away.

He had just barely broken through Shannon's prickly outer shell. He couldn't expect to accomplish everything in one day—or night—no matter how sweet that night had been.

"Okay, let's call it quits for the day. I won't push you for answers, but please don't push me away. What happened last night between us was beautiful. You can take it as slowly as you want, but at some point, you're going to have to tell me what bothers you so much about this particular spell. And you're going to have to be ready and willing to use it if necessary. I need to know that you will fight back if you are in danger."

CHAPTER 33

Winnie Thorne stood outside the door to Baubles and Beads, debating with herself. Should she or should she not go in? Something was going on in this store. She knew it. She'd had a feeling several times, either as she passed the store or when talking about things with her cousin and his partner. Until now, however, she'd dismissed it. But since the conversation with Dave and Shannon a few days before the big engagement party, she'd been sure her suspicions were correct. She'd watched Shannon and Dave come out of the store that day, suddenly acting like lovers when a few minutes before while talking with her and Abby it hadn't been the case at all.

Yes, she'd been pretty sure that Dave was interested in Shannon, but no way did things happen that fast—and in the middle of a boutique, no less. The sudden change had to have something to do with the Artificial Witch Murders. She just knew it. And she was going to find out just exactly what it was. Her childhood friend had been killed after all, and despite what everyone said, Winnie felt as if she had helped to set Ashley on the path that led to her death.

She took a deep breath and entered the store. The bells that hung over the door tinkled as she entered, announcing the arrival of a customer. No one came out of the back right away though, so Winnie quietly walked around, looking at everything. She'd been in a few times, talking with Salvia or Harrison. They'd needed some help when they first moved in, and she'd been glad to carry a few boxes or arrange things on the shelves. She hadn't managed to come by the store, though, since they'd been fully stocked and open. It was a good excuse.

Salvia had done a nice job arranging her products throughout the store. It definitely had a retro 70's vibe going on, from the classic Andy Warhol print of the Beatles and the vibrant, neon swirl of Peter Max posters on the wall to the fragrance of patchouli. It looked a lot like the way her grandmother described how things had been in the Haight-Ashbury section of San Francisco back in the day.

Winnie could appreciate the vibe. She always enjoyed those stories. Her grandmother, Delilah, had not only been a witch, but a flower child. She'd protested for peace. That's where she'd met Winnie's grandfather, Douglas Thorne. They'd fallen in love, married, and come back to his hometown of Rivelou, where they were now continuing to live happily ever after, just two witches with a couple of witch children and grandchildren to spoil.

Winnie found herself drawn to the Tarot cards in the back corner of the store. She'd always done well using them. Her favorite set was rather worn; maybe she could get a deck, just to allay suspicions about why she was here.

At that moment, Harrison came out of the back room, startling her.

"Oh!" she said, dropping the deck she'd been looking at and immediately bending down to pick up the cards that had spilled from their box all over the floor. "I'm sorry, Harrison, I was just looking at these cards. So clumsy of me."

She was babbling, and she knew it. Harrison would be suspicious if she didn't get it together quickly.

"Hi Winnie, were you looking for something in particular?" he asked and bent down to help her with the mess she had made.

"Not really, just killing time. Abby doesn't expect me in for work for another half hour or so, and I just didn't feel like going in early. I'm so sorry again for the mess."

She picked up the last of the cards and handed them to Harrison. She blushed when he held her hand for a minute as he took them. He was as old as her cousin Dave, for the goddess' sake. He had to be at least 30! Harrison had always been a little odd, though, so she just put it down to that. Maybe he was just one of those neurodivergent people who didn't pick up on social cues well.

"Don't worry. No harm, no foul," he said. He let go of her hand finally, then looked at the package he was holding.

"Are you interested in the Tarot?"

"Yeah, a little I guess."

"Any idea how to use them?" he asked.

"Oh, uh, not really."

She knew better than to say anything about already owning three packs and that she'd been thinking about buying another. Or that she was already considered a skilled reader by her coven, despite being only twenty. She was here undercover, after all. She took a breath and quieted her nerves. Dave was going to fuss when he found out what she'd been up to, but if she learned anything that would help solve the murders, it would be worth it.

"Let me show you." He guided her over to the counter, fanned the cards, closed the deck again, and then handed them to her. "I've been playing around with them a little since Salvia got them for the store. I think I'm getting pretty good at them. Now, we're going to do just a simple reading so you can get an idea of how they work. First, you shuffle them."

After she had done as he asked, he took the cards from her and shuffled them one more time. Winnie tried to keep her face impassive; he'd just mixed his energy with hers. The reading he got would be mixed now, a part of it coming from his energy and a part of it from hers.

"Now we're going to pick three cards, one to represent your past, one for your present, and one for your future."

Well, that much was correct, she thought as he fanned the cards with a flourish and motioned to her to choose one. She pulled The Sun, represented in this deck as a bright yellow ball with a happy face, surrounded by flowers.

"This is The Sun card," he said. "And since you pulled it thinking about your past, you obviously had a happy childhood."

Should she say something? Express awe at his skill or the correctness of his guess? She didn't know what to do, so she just nodded and said nothing. Harrison didn't seem to notice.

"Okay, lay that card down here." He indicated a spot on the counter. "Now pick another card and put it next to The Sun; we'll see what that shows us."

Winnie kept her eyes on the deck rather than looking at Harrison. Would he consider it flirting if she did look him in the eyes? Oh yuck! She certainly didn't want him to think that! She kept her head down, drew the second card, and handed it to the man.

"The Five of Cups. That stands for sorrow in your present." He laid the card next to The Sun.

"That makes sense. My friend Ashley was one of the girls killed in the Artificial Witch Murders."

This time she looked at him as she spoke. She wanted to know how he reacted. Would he show anxiety?

"Wow, I didn't know one of them was a friend of yours," he said, his face blank. "That's too bad; I'm sorry for your loss. Of course it makes sense you would draw the card for sorrow right now." He put his hand over hers again, presumably in sympathy.

She took a deep breath and withdrew it discreetly. "Yeah, it's been a really bad time for all of us. Ashley was in my high school graduation class. It's really sad, you know?" How did Dave and Shannon do this? It was so hard to act normally when she felt as if her every thought were being laid bare for this man, and he knew exactly what she was thinking.

That was silly, however. Harrison couldn't read her thoughts. Yes, she could feel he had some power, but he seemed so oblivious to it she couldn't believe he was trained as a mind reader.

"Well, let's see if we can conjure up some good times for your future. I just get feelings sometimes, you know? And I've got a feeling great things are coming for you. Salvia tells me I have the Sight. I'm not sure I believe that, but I do know I can tell that there are great things in your future, Winnie."

"I hope so. This past year hasn't been the greatest. I need something to look forward to right now." This wasn't an exaggeration. She really did need something good to happen soon.

"Well, let's see what we can do for you." He fanned the cards again with a flourish, like an old school dealer at a carnival show.

Winnie chose one more card, although now she wasn't sure whose future it would show. Harrison's energy was all over this deck. Was she drawing his future or hers?

She turned up the card for him to see and they both turned pale: XIII—the Grim Reaper. She hurriedly placed the card on the table, then wiped her hand on her jeans.

"The Grim Reaper. It doesn't have to mean death, you know," Harrison said kindly.

But what if it did? And was it foretelling her death—or his?

The chime rang over the door again, interrupting them. Salvia bustled in.

"Harrison," she called as she entered, apparently not seeing them at the far end of the counter.

"Hey, over here." Harrison hastily gathered the cards and slipped them in their box.

"Oh, you startled me," said Salvia.

"It seems to be what I'm best at today," he said with a grin.

"What do you mean?" she asked.

"Oh, he just startled me when I came in the store a little while ago," explained Winnie.

"Oh, Winnie, I hadn't noticed you there." Salvia walked around to the other side of the counter, gave Harrison a long kiss, and put her arm around his waist as if to claim him.

What was it with these people? Did they really think she was going to find an old guy like Harrison sexy?

"Did you want to buy something?"

"Harrison was just showing me the Tarot cards. I think I'll take them. They have instructions, right?" Winnie asked, back in her part of the novice Tarot reader.

"Yes, of course. I'll wrap them up for you."

"Thanks, see you around," she said as soon as she had paid her money. She stuffed the cards in her pocket, still bothered as she thought about the weird vibe in the store. Was it Harrison or Salvia who gave her the creeps? Maybe it was both. She stood lost in thought on the sidewalk when she heard someone call, "Hey, Winnie, I thought that was you."

It was Tyler, standing on the sidewalk with some of his friends.

Tyler was a good guy. She'd spent much of the party last weekend hanging out with him. There hadn't been too many people their age, so it was nice to have someone she knew well to hang together, dancing and talking.

They'd had a lot of fun. He was a great dancer, but she'd known him since high school, and they'd never been any more than friends. He was a shapeshifter, a wolf in fact. Sometimes the wolves and witches and the other paranormals in her high school had banded into cliques, each faction ignoring the other. But Tyler was one of those people who seemed to get along with everyone. Now he introduced her to the friends who were with him.

"Hey, this is Ryan," he said, pointing to a tall, gangly guy with red hair and freckles. "And this is Damon." More compact than either Tyler or Ryan, Damon had muscles that spoke of a lot of time spent in the gym. Or maybe he was on one of the sports teams? At any rate, Winnie looked him over appreciatively. He had dark, curly hair and deep brown eyes with a soulful look that seemed to see her deepest thoughts. Winnie shivered, but she didn't want the guys to know.

"Do you all go to U of R, too?" she asked.

Damon, it turned out, was also a business major, like Winnie. "I want to help my family with their business when I get out of college," he explained.

"Hey, I'm taking business classes, too. Maybe I'll see you around."

"That would be cool," he said.

As the trio left, Winnie stared after them. Maybe she was going to get lucky, after all. Damon seemed really nice—and very hot. That last Tarot card must have been for Harrison, she thought. Not for her.

CHAPTER 34

Shannon stood in the locker room of the station, arms up as her partner attached a wire inside her bra.

"You're going to be careful tonight, right?" Dave asked for the thousandth time. In fact, it wasn't really a question, more a command.

"Yes, I'm going to be careful. This is just an initial meeting. I really don't expect anything to happen. I'm just going to learn who all the players are. It may not be Salvia, you know. It may be someone else in this group."

"I'd bet $1,000 bucks on it being Salvia and not one of her little empowerment seekers. Who goes to this shit anyway?"

"Women need all the help they can get in the world of men. Especially women don't have the aid of magic."

At that moment Chief Anderson knocked on the locker room door. "You ready in there, Shannon?" he asked.

"Yep, good to go," she said, and pulled her t-shirt on. The spring had continued to be warm, and now in late May it was easily t-shirt and shorts weather in the evenings.

Dave admired the way the shirt clung to her breasts and the way the short shorts showed off her long legs. He reminded himself the meeting was supposed to be for women only. At least he didn't have to worry about anyone else trying to hit on her when he wasn't around to protect her.

"Since Tony's monitoring your mic tonight, maybe I can drop you by the store, see if Harrison wants to come out for a beer," he said. Making sure the man wasn't anywhere near his woman seemed like a very good idea, especially when she was dressed like that. Not to mention, it would be good to try once again to get some more detailed information from Harrison on just what Salvia was into.

"That's a good idea, Dave," said Chief Anderson, coming into the room. "I want both of you to remember you're just looking for information right now. Talk to people; get a feel for things and get a list of the other people in this group. Maybe we can squeeze some of them for information. And Dave, do not do anything stupid. Shannon's an experienced cop. You're there to drop her off just to see if you can gain this Harrison guy's trust—not to get in Shannon's way."

"Yes, Sir."

At that moment, Jake and Tony popped in the locker room.

"Shannon, we have faith in you. Get us some leads so we can arrest the people involved in these murders," Tony said.

"Go get 'em, girl," added Jake, patting her on the shoulder.

"Wow!" Shannon said as they left the building and headed for her car. "They really do trust me. I never thought it would happen."

"Of course they trust you; they see that you're good at what you do," replied Dave.

"That wasn't how it was just a few weeks ago."

"Remember what I told you about letting them in? Telling them the truth and allowing them to get to know you?"

"Yeah, don't get hurt patting yourself on the back," she laughed as they headed out of the parking lot.

~~~

"Hey, you interested in grabbing a drink while the ladies are doing their thing?" Dave asked Harrison when they arrived at the store a few minutes before the scheduled meeting.

"Sounds good, man. Just give me a sec to get my stuff from the back room."

He came out a minute later with his bike helmet and gave Salvia a kiss. "I'll see you later. Enjoy your meeting. Dave, I'll follow you."

They headed to a bar out on the highway. Dave had thought it was far enough out of town that he wouldn't be recognized. That hope died the minute they entered the bar.

"Hey, Dave, how you doing? You up for some pool?" called Joe Lessing, a neighbor of Chris and Ana. He'd first met the man when Ana was attacked by a dog the year before. It had later turned out that the animal was actually a werewolf—Alexander Fontaine to be precise—but no one knew that at the time. Joe, a non-para, still didn't.

"How's business? Things quiet in town?" Joe asked him now.

"Oh, the usual," Dave said. "This is my friend, Harrison. He owns that new store over near the university."

"Oh, so you're the one who's tempting my wife to spend all that money," Joe said, with a mock scowl. "She loves your place." He and Harrison shook hands.

"Maybe we'll give you a run at pool after we get a beer," Dave said.

"So what do you do?" Harrison asked when they'd found a place at the bar. "I never asked."

It was lucky, Dave thought, that he and Shannon had decided not to hide their professions. Rivelou was a small town after all, and as the meeting with Joe just now showed, it was too likely he'd run into someone who recognized him, either as a cop, a witch, or both.

"Oh, I thought you knew. I'm a cop," said Dave.

"Yeah, really? That's cool. I didn't know that. Any interesting cases you've been on lately?"

They chatted casually about the town for a few minutes as Dave came up with a few harmless and amusing stories to tell Harrison. He tried to turn the conversation to baseball—the St. Louis Cardinals were already doing well this season—but Harrison kept bringing the conversation back to the job.

"Hey, do you know anything about these Artificial Witch Murders I keep reading about on the internet?"

Dave had to walk a fine line between getting information from Harrison while not giving away too much. "I really can't say too much about an ongoing investigation. But we are chasing down some leads." That was the line they'd agreed on. It sounded official. Maybe Dave would be able to give Harrison just enough information to feel as if he were special without telling him anything the general public didn't already know.

"Yeah, what type of leads? Anything more than I'm hearing on the news?"

Yep, Dave thought, Harrison was playing right into his hands. Out loud he said, "Well, I really shouldn't be saying this, but we do think the murderer is someone who's playing around with witchcraft but doesn't really know what it's all about. She—or maybe it's more than one person—is pretending to be a witch."

"You don't believe in all this supernatural B.S., do you? You talk like you think it's real," Harrison said.

Dave laughed. "You're the one with the shop that sells books on curses and necromancy, remember?"

"Well, yeah, but like I said, that's all Salvia. I let her do what makes her happy. This witch stuff, it's a girl thing, ya' know? Like this empowerment stuff she does—the big meeting once a week—it's just women wanting a night out away from their guys, right? I don't get it; I'm here having a beer with you. Big deal. But women just can't be honest about wanting a night out. They have to disguise it and pretend it's something important. This witchcraft thing, now; I'm sure you think it's as much a ball of crap as I do." He looked intently at Dave as he made the comment.

"Mm," Dave said and nodded, not knowing what to say.

"Yeah, you just have to let them have their little fun; then, you snap your fingers and reel in the leash.

Dave was having a hard time not showing his disdain for some of the man's sexist attitudes, not to mention his attitude about witches. He probably thought all witches were women. Dave would love to use the fire spell with Harrison right now, open his hand an show him a ball of flame, just to see what he would do.

It would be a lot of fun but wouldn't help solve the murders. Instead, he bit his tongue. Coming out with, "I'm a witch," here in the middle of a bar was not a wise move. He didn't want to out himself, not to mention his friends. He'd be in serious trouble with High Priestess Cassandra. And his boss. And Hank Bertrand. No, that was not a wise idea. He tuned back into Harrison's monologue.

"Now look at Salvia," the man was saying. "She likes to play pretend witch and if that makes her happy, so be it. But you and I know better, don't we? Despite what we may see on the Net. It's a crazy place, the internet. All sorts of weird and secret things you can find if you just have enough juice to get there, ya' know?"

"What do you mean?" Was Harrison saying that he realized that Dave had power? Was he saying he'd been on PackNet? Or was it just that the man thought witchcraft wasn't real and was blowing smoke?

"You know, just like the store. I told her she could use my money for it as long as she doesn't lose too much. I give her strict limits, ya' know?"

"So the store is really yours, not Salvia's?"

"Right. I'm the one backing it. I just let her play around with it to keep her happy. Then I get to do my thing, too."

CHAPTER 35

"Head on into the back room," Salvia told Shannon as Dave and Harrison left. "A few of the girls are here already. I'm just waiting to let a couple more in."

Shannon did as suggested and entered the back room. It was obviously a storeroom, but the boxes and assorted items for the front of the store had been draped in black and silver cloths to make the room feel cozier and more finished. There were about a dozen folding chairs placed in a circle with a small table at the center. It held candles, several crystals, some bowls filled with herbs, and a larger, empty bowl made of brass. An incense burner on the table was already lit, and it filled the room with Salvia's signature patchouli scent. Quiet, relaxing nature sounds played on an unseen speaker in the background. The recording cycled through light rain, to birds chirping, to the sound of the ocean. It was kind of relaxing, Shannon admitted to herself, feeling some of the tension in her shoulders start to ease. The atmosphere was a mix of tawdry and cozy. Salvia obviously wanted to decorate as if she were hosting a sophisticated party, but the room just didn't manage to come off that way.

There was nothing wrong with displaying her goods for sale. She was here to make money, after all. But somehow the mix just didn't work. The relaxing bath salts sat next to a display of some of the woman's darker magic books and a couple of Voodoo dolls. The elegant wooden trays were next to some Halloween décor paper cats. The whole thing was rather like the woman herself, a mix of the stereotype of a television witch combined with Salvia's natural charisma.

The overhead lights had been turned off, and the room was lit only by candles that sat on some larger tables in two separate corners of the room, both draped with black and silver cloths similar to the ones on the walls. On the larger table sat books, Tarot cards, herbs, bath salts, and other items that Salvia sold in her store. The other table held a couple of plates of cookies, a pot with hot water, and a variety of herbal tea bags.

"Hi, I'm Shannon." She introduced herself to two of the five women who were already standing by the refreshment table, drinking tea from insulated paper cups. They introduced themselves as Mollie and Emma. They were both in their early thirties, dressed much as Shannon was in t-shirts and shorts. As they talked, Shannon learned they were both moms with young children at home. The other three women, Ava, Olivia, and Grace, had obviously just come from work and were still wearing their skirts and high heels. A few other, younger, women came in, probably college students Shannon guessed by their age, but Salvia still had not entered. Shannon assumed they were waiting for at least one more person.

Finally, the woman came through the door, talking to someone who was following her. Shannon's mouth fell open when she saw who it was.

"Winnie, what are you doing here?" She cursed herself even as she spoke. She shouldn't have appeared so startled.

The girl was also surprised at the sight of Shannon but hid it well after her first shocked reaction.

"Salvia told me about her group, and I thought it could be really good for me," she said. "I've been having a hard time the last few weeks." Only someone who knew her well would have caught the tremble in her voice.

"Shannon, I'd forgotten you know Abby well, so of course you've met Winnie," Salvia said brightly. Thank goodness she apparently had not noticed Shannon's and Winnie's reactions to each other.

"Yes, we've met at the store," Shannon replied, giving Winnie a look she hoped the girl would understand meant she should not say anything about Dave being her cousin. Or any other closer relationship with Shannon.

Winnie gave a barely perceptible nod.

"Alright ladies, let's sit down and start our meeting."

There were a few moments of friendly chaos as everyone got their tea and cookies and found a seat. Shannon made sure to sit across the room from Winnie.

Salvia stood by the table in the center of the room. "I'm

so glad to see you all here tonight," she said when everyone was seated. "Let's start by everyone introducing themselves—just your first name please—and a power word that reflects your current aspirations. For example, I'm Salvia, and my word this week is 'dynamic.'"

They went around the room, and as each woman introduced herself and gave her one-word affirmation, Shannon tried to memorize something about their faces and features. It was going to be hard tracking them down if she only had first names. How many Emma's, Jessica's, and Ashley's were there in the area? Rivelou wasn't Chicago, by any means, but it wasn't that small, either.

Maybe she could ask Winnie if she knew some of these people, particularly the college students. She quickly dismissed that idea. Dave was going to be livid at the girl when he found out she had been here. Winnie was lucky that he was her cousin, not her father, and didn't have the power to ground her, Shannon thought with amusement. If he did, Winnie wouldn't be leaving home for the next twenty years.

She tried to pay attention to the power words each of the women came up with, wondering if they could give her clues as to who might be involved in the killings. "Courage," "transformation," and "tranquility" seemed to be the favorites of the group. When it was Winnie's turn, however, her word was "sorrow."

Shannon wanted to reach out and hold the girl's hand, but she couldn't; she didn't want anyone to know they were anything other than casual acquaintances.

Salvia responded to Winnie's choice of word with a little frown. Did she not have enough empathy to handle someone who was experiencing true grief? Was this group supposed to only deal with good feelings, not the sad, messy parts of life?

The woman hurried them into what was apparently the main event of the evening, a small ritual where each person was given a piece of paper on which to write down their intentions for the coming week.

"Tonight, we honor the power that flows within each of us," she said in a self-important voice. She lit a small fire in the brass bowl, and as each of the women came up to the table and dropped their papers in, the light flared a different color. The women seemed impressed.

Shannon followed suit and pretended to be amazed also. She noticed Winnie did the same. "Good girl, Winnie. You aren't too bad at this undercover stuff," she said to herself silently. The color change was just a cheap parlor trick. Salvia obviously had some chemicals in her hand that she was surreptitiously throwing into the bowl as she "blessed" each woman's intention.

"Our strength grows when we acknowledge both our shadows and our light," she recited once all the papers had burned to ash.

Shannon wanted to stick around after the meeting to have a chance to talk to some of the women and find out more about them, but Winnie was hurrying toward the door. She followed her. If Dave were outside, she wanted to try to head off any public confrontation.

"Please don't tell Dave," Winnie begged as they walked outside into the warm spring air together. But Shannon didn't even have time to answer. Just at that moment Dave drove up in Shannon's car, Harrison following on his Ducati.

CHAPTER 36

Dave's mouth gaped open when he saw Winnie walked out of the store with Shannon. He quickly got out of the car, obviously planning to start questioning her.

Shannon made a quick chopping motion with her hand, telling Dave to keep quiet. She came up to him and gave him a kiss. "Don't say anything in front of Harrison," she whispered.

Dave took a deep breath and nodded. He kissed her back, whispering, "What the hell is going on?"

"I'll explain later." She turned to Winnie. "Good night Winnie, it was good to get to know you better. Maybe I'll see you next week." She waved and headed to the passenger side of her car, pulling Dave along with her. Winnie gave a wave and headed quickly toward the back of the lot where the employees parked. She was just happy to get away without her cousin chastising her.

Harrison had watched the entire encounter, Shannon noticed. "Say something to him," she mouthed to Dave.

His mouth slimmed to a tight line, but he turned and waved to the man. "Hey, maybe we can do this again next week," he called and headed around to the driver's side of the car, not waiting for an answer.

As soon as both the doors were closed, he started the car so fast he ground the gears. "What the hell is going on?" he demanded, backing the vehicle into traffic.

"If you don't calm down, you're going to cause an accident," Shannon said. "As far as I know, Winnie being there was perfectly innocent. She's been feeling down since her friend was murdered, and Salvia invited her to the group as a way to cheer her up."

"But she's just a kid. Why would Salvia…"

"She's just as old as the three girls who were killed, and there were several other college age girls there tonight, also."

"I've got to tell her…"

"Dave, you'll tell your cousin nothing," a voice sounded

in both of their ears.

"Damnit, I forgot we were wearing earpieces," said Dave.

"Good thing it didn't get hot and heavy with you two then," Tony's voice chuckled. "The chief's here with me. He says to get your asses back to the department ASAP."

~~~

At headquarters the chief, Tony, Jake Waseaux, and, surprisingly, Nathan Lazard were waiting for them. Dave raised his eyebrows when he saw the coroner there but knew better than to question his presence.

"So how did it go?" the chief asked as they sat down. "Shannon, we could hear you, but Dave, you only had an earpiece, no mic, so you could hear us but not the other way around. Did you learn anything interesting from this Harrison character?"

"Interesting? Maybe. If we can figure out what it means. He was kind of speaking in riddles. Like saying something vague, then giving me a 'wink, wink, nod, nod' thing, like he was telling me we were both in on the same joke."

"What exactly did he talk about?" asked the chief.

"I think he's been on PackNet or at least knows about it."

That statement fell like a bomb in the room. There was an explosion of noise as everyone spoke at once.

Dr. Lazard's voice overrode the others. "I've told Hank his grand scheme to bring paranormals together was going to bring us all down!"

"Enough! Everyone, calm down," said the chief. "Dave, what exactly were his words?"

"It wasn't so much what he said as how he said it. Let me think... He said, 'It's a crazy place, the internet. All sorts of weird and secret things you can find if you just have enough juice to get there.' That's it. It wasn't so much what he said as his attitude, his expression. I almost felt it was a threat."

"You're sure he has power?" asked Waseaux, "I've never met him. Without it, he shouldn't be able to access PackNet. Maybe he's just blowing smoke."

Shannon and Dave both nodded. They'd both met him. They were sure.

"And did he say anything else important?"

"Well, he's a bit of a sexist, that's for sure, and if he's telling the truth, he's the one who funded the store. It's his money, not Salvia's, according to him. And he said by letting Salvia have the money 'to play around with the store'..." Dave said, using air quotes. "He gets the time to do his own thing."

"Well, being sexist isn't an admirable quality, but it's not a crime either," said Tony. "So Shannon, what did you learn that might not have come over the mic—and what was Dave's cousin doing there?"

"Well to the first part of your question, I didn't learn anything that points to one particular person there being involved in the murder. There were about a dozen women, ranging from late teens like Winnie to mid-thirties—I didn't get last names for most of them. They all just seemed to be there to take a night off and relax, be with friends, and refresh themselves. There was no talk of witchcraft, power, magic, spells. Nothing. Not even the murders."

"Salvia did have some of her books out for sale along with some of her other things, but she didn't push anything in particular. The most she did was to have some chemicals in her hand to make the fire burn different colors when everyone put the papers with their intentions written on them in the bowl. It was a cheap trick; I spotted it easily, and I think some of the others did, too."

"And what about Winnie?" asked Dave. You still haven't told me what she was doing there."

"She knows Salvia from working at Abby's shop right next door. She said Salvia invited her because she knew she's been depressed lately. When she came in, I motioned for her not to say she knew me, but it was too late. Salvia already realized we had to know each other. We both played it off like I'd just met her while shopping in the store and didn't know her any better than that. She did good, Dave. She didn't give me away."

"I don't want her going back."

"I don't think that's up to you."

"That's right," said the chief. "Dave, I know how you feel, but she's of age and you can't stop her from going to a meeting if she wants to go."

"I can warn…"

"No!" the chief said sharply. "You can't warn her. Yes, I just said she's of age, but she's also inexperienced, and she might give something away without meaning to. The less she knows the better. Let it go for now. With luck, she won't go back, and we won't have to worry about her."

"I want to get back to this PackNet business," said Lazard. "I think we need a meeting with Bertrand and his wolves. They were the ones who started PackNet. If it's been compromised, they need to be the ones to fix it."

"Yes, you're right. I'll set up a meeting for the three of us," the chief said. It was obvious that anyone less senior than those three would not be invited to the meeting.

As the meeting broke up, Lazard took a minute to stop Shannon. "I'm happy to see that you listened to my tale and are no longer closing yourself off to new love."

Shannon smiled at him. "Thank you; a lot of people have been pushing me to open myself up. It's helped."

"If you ever need someone to talk to, you know where to find me."

The doctor left after promising the chief some files that were needed on an old case, and Dave came up and put a possessive hand on her back. "What did he want?"

"He was just being nice. And by the way, you need to thank him. He was the first person who encouraged me to open up to you."

"Hmm, maybe I do owe him a thank you, then." He gave her a quick kiss. "Let's get out of here. Your place or mine tonight?"

CHAPTER 37

As the next few weeks went by, Shannon and Dave fell into a routine. They split their free time between her house in town and his out in the country. Dave continued with the magic lessons for Shannon although they avoided any talk of *Incantare Thanatos* or any other defensive magic. That topic sat between them like an elephant under the rug. It ate at Shannon. She wanted to explain to David why she hated that spell. She knew he was curious. But when he found out her secret, would he still look at her the same way? Would he want to touch her? To kiss her? To make love to her?

She was afraid, and it colored everything she did.

On the job, they switched back from nights to days. It made it easier to connect with their friends and family. The night before the Summer Solstice they scheduled dinner at The Strawberry Moon, in the small river town of Grey Stone, with her brother and Ana. They all headed out there on a lovely evening in early June.

The drive through the country was relaxing. The food was supposed to be marvelous, according to Ana, who had eaten there many times since it was owned by a fellow shapeshifter and friend of her grandparents, Marianne Legato. Shannon was ready for a relaxing evening where she didn't have to think about anything. When they arrived at the restaurant, they received celebrity treatment.

"Ana and Chris, it's so good to see you again," the older woman said, kissing them both on the cheeks. "I so enjoyed your engagement party."

Ana introduced Dave and Shannon, who received hugs and kisses from Miz Marianne. "You're family now, and don't forget it," she told Shannon when she tried to pull away. She wasn't sure she'd ever get used to the easy acceptance and friendship that was offered in this town. Too bad she had ignored it for the first year she lived here.

They settled at a table with a river view, and the waiter brought them cocktails and appetizers. They made their dinner choices—pecan chicken for Shannon, blackened Creole shrimp for Dave and Chris, and a ribeye for Ana. "My wolf needs her red meat," Chris joked.

Shannon tried her best to keep the conversation light, but with a werewolf, a Hunter, and two witches out to dinner together, the talk inevitably turned to the paranormal, particularly because they knew they were in a safe place. The Strawberry Moon was guarded by strong protection and privacy spells.

"I can't believe Winnie is still going to those damn empowerment meetings," said Dave.

"I'm starting to think there's nothing going on there. I keep on going, but so far everything is totally innocent. Nothing that Salvia has done indicates she's interested in dark magic, at all," Shannon told him, putting her hand on Dave's arm. She knew how much Winnie's attending the meetings worried him.

"I know we haven't found anything, but there's something just not right about those two. I feel it in my gut," he replied.

"You haven't found anything new out from Harrison, either?" asked Chris.

"Not a word. He makes me uncomfortable, though, with all these veiled references to what he's learned on the internet. Some of the stuff has to have come from PackNet. There's no place else he could learn it. I feel like he's teasing me with it."

"I was invited to a meeting yesterday with your grandfather, Ana, as well as Cassandra, Chief Anderson, and Dr. Lazard," Chris said.

Shannon was grateful for what she thought was a change of subject. Unfortunately, her gratitude was short-lived.

"Let me guess, more about PackNet," said Dave.

"You got it in one. Anderson and Lazard want to shut it down."

"No!" cried Ana. "It's too useful to every one of us. We've come to rely on it."

"And that's the problem. Too many paranormals are using it, and that makes it vulnerable to hacking."

"But no one from outside the paranormal community could be hacking into PackNet, or we'd be seeing new things on the rest of the internet that referred to paranormals. That hasn't happened, has it?" asked Dave.

"Not that we know of. Gabe has been keeping an eye out, but as of now there's been nothing out there in the rest of the world about big discoveries regarding werewolves, or vampires, or anything new and different in the paranormal world other than the usual, mostly inaccurate, stuff."

Gabe, who was also Marianne's grandson, had been friends with Ana and her brother Dan since high school when he'd shown an ability in coding. He had combined it with spells and incantations to create something new, then taken the idea to their pack leader. Hank had agreed that connecting the many paranormal communities that existed throughout the world through a combination of modern technology and powerful magic could benefit everyone. And in the last fifteen years it had worked without a problem.

PackNet had brought paranormals together, no matter where they lived, or their species or magical abilities. It had certainly benefited Chris, who had gained respect worldwide in his work as a detective of sorts, policing the paranormals who stepped out of line. PackNet benefited everyone, but there had always been a danger it would be hacked by non-paras, and their world would be outed.

"But now, Gabe is telling me there's evidence that PackNet has been hacked, Chris continued.

Shannon put down her fork. The moist and flavorful chicken she was eating suddenly tasted like ashes in her mouth. "Who would have that kind of knowledge—not to mention that kind of power?"

"Gabe thinks it may be more than one person—one person who is technically savvy and another with the power."

"And you think Harrison and Saliva...?"

"One, or the other, or both. We aren't sure yet," said Chris. "But Ana's right; PackNet has become invaluable. If someone's hacked it, we're all at risk.

"Who would want to do that, though?" asked Ana.

"Anyone with the ability to get into PackNet should have a vested interest in keeping the non-para's unaware of it, and the knowledge a secret."

"You'd think that, but there are always bad actors who think they can turn something that is good and benefits everyone into something that is only for their own gain," said Dave.

"And you think Harrison and Salvia might be those bad actors? Are you sure Harrison has enough power to access PackNet?" asked Ana.

"I'm sure. I can feel his power; I just don't know what his specific area is. He's not a shifter, of that I'm certain. Some type of witchcraft abilities is my best guess. And it seems to be growing."

"I agree," said Shannon. "When I first met him, I could barely feel his power, and now every time I see him, he seems stronger. He's either very good at cloaking his power, or he's totally unaware of it."

"Are you sure Salvia isn't the one with the power?" questioned Chris.

"I feel like we just keep going around in circles," complained Shannon in response. "If Harrison knows he has power, is he the one who has hacked PackNet? If he has power but isn't aware of it, how would he even know to look for PackNet? If Salvia has no power, is she the one who murdered the three girls? Or was that Harrison? Or someone else entirely? My head starts to hurt just thinking about it."

"Let me give you another theory," Chris said.

Shannon groaned.

"I know how you feel, but you need to hear this, Shannon. What if Harrison has just enough power that some other paranormal has tapped into him and is using him?"

"You mean like…"

Chris nodded solemnly; Ana and Dave looked at the brother and sister, confused.

"But that's not possible," Shannon said.

"Are you sure? She's done it before. Just because we haven't heard anything about her doesn't mean…"

"No! No! It's not possible. I…"

"You what, Shannon? I never asked you about that night." Chris's voice took on a sharp edge that had Dave throwing his napkin on the table and starting to stand up to confront the other man. "Why are you upsetting your sister? Whatever you're thinking, there's no need to be so harsh with her."

Chris started to reply, but Ana put her hands out toward both of them, as if to keep them from saying anything they would later regret.

Chris continued. "I think there is a need to be harsh—and honest. I'm sorry Shannon, but you have to come clean now. There are good reasons for it."

Shannon took a deep breath. "Maybe you're right, but not here. I don't care how many protections spells there are here, this needs to be private. Let's go back to my place."

They finished their dinners in strained silence. Dave and Ana tried to make small talk while Chris and Shannon were silent. Shannon just pushed her meal around her plate, unable to eat anything more.

When they finally paid for the meal and headed through the now dark parking lot, Dave suddenly stopped and put a hand on Shannon's shoulder. "Do you feel that?" he asked.

Shannon and Chris stopped and looked around. Chris immediately put his arm around Ana. As a shifter, she held a different sort of power. This was not her area of expertise, and Chris knew she might be vulnerable. "Someone is out there," he said.

"Do you recognize who it is?" asked Shannon.

"No, do you?"

"No. I... I don't think so. It doesn't feel exactly like..." she answered hesitantly.

"Come on, let's just get in the car and head back to Shannon's; then, the two of you can fill Ana and me in on what this is all about," said Dave. They hurried into Chris's SUV and headed home.

CHAPTER 38

At Shannon's house they got their coffee and settled comfortably in the living room. Shannon was reminded of another time when she, Chris, and Ana had sat here. It had been morning then, and Chris and Ana had come to tell her they thought they had found the shifter who had killed her husband, Jason. Did all hard conversations have to take place here? She shivered. Her beloved home suddenly felt less safe.

Dave sat down beside her and put his arm around her. She relaxed against him, enjoying the sensation. Would it be the last time he wanted to comfort and protect her? He was so good. He was a protector. Just like her brother. She wasn't. What she had done hadn't been about protecting others. She was an avenger. She had avenged Jason, and she had avenged the victims of the crimes her mother had committed.

She took a deep breath. Everyone was looking at her, waiting for her to start.

"You remember the night you left home, Chris?"

"Of course. I'd just graduated from high school. I had a bad fight with Mother and she told me to leave and never come back. Said I was useless. I packed my bags and got out of there as fast as I could. I was afraid she'd change her mind and bring me back. Force me to stay." He shivered now just thinking about it, and Ana took his hand in hers.

"You were right to get out so quickly. After you left, she called me into her workroom. Said we needed to protect ourselves from you. That you might tell others about us, put us in danger."

"She never meant put herself in danger. I'd never have done anything that could have hurt you, and she knew that. And if that meant keeping Mother's secrets, so be it," said Chris.

"I know that—I knew it at the time. I begged Mother to listen, but she wanted to bind you. Not just bind your powers—bind you. She had a place ready for you. Said because you were her son, she couldn't kill you. She had that much maternal feeling, I guess. She wouldn't kill you outright. But she could stop you.

She was preparing to use *Incantare Thanatos* on you and then…"

"But you said Chris had left. How was she going to do it?" interrupted Dave. "That spell requires you to be within sight of the person you're using it on. You can't just work it on anyone, anywhere. That wouldn't be right."

"She'd found a way. She was brilliant at spells. She wrote it all down in a book. She could have bound Chris, then taken her time finding him. It wouldn't have been hard for her."

Ana looked pale. So did Chris. He reached out to Ana and put his arm around her shoulders, to comfort her or himself, Shannon wasn't sure. It didn't matter that it had been ten years ago. Finding out your mother had planned to kill you—even indirectly—couldn't be easy.

"I knew what I had to do. As she prepared the spell, I turned it on her. It rebounded and I was able to stop her. She fell at my feet. She couldn't move. Only her eyes. She stared at me with such hate." Shannon shivered at the memory.

"I didn't know what to do. I called Jason. Who else would I call?"

"Shannon, you could have called me. You knew I had my cellphone. We'd set up a way for you to get in touch with me. I would have come."

"I was afraid for you. Afraid of what she could still do to you even though I'd bound her." Shannon took a deep breath and continued. "Jason came over at once. I showed him what I'd done, and he helped me."

"Of course he did. He knew our mother was evil, and he would have done anything he could for you, Shannon, you know that."

Dave felt as if he were sitting in the audience watching a play being performed. He heard everything Shannon and Chris said. Mentally he understood the words. But emotionally? He felt ill. Without even thinking he moved away from Shannon and put his head in his hands. He didn't want to think about these two kids—that's what they'd been at the time—younger even than Winnie was right now. They'd been forced into an impossible situation. He wanted to cry for them. He wanted to go back in time and kill Beatrix Spier. He felt a hot flash of jealousy, too, for Jason, the man who had been there for Shannon. The man who had loved her first. He had been a teenager, too, but he had been there when she needed help the most.

What was wrong with him that he could be jealous of a dead man? He shook off the feeling and reached out to Shannon again.

"No, Dave, don't touch me now. I can't bear it until you hear everything. Then, if you can still look at me, it'll be okay."

"Alright, let's hear the rest. What did you and Jason do? Did you kill her? Don't expect me to criticize you for it. She wanted to torture her own son. Right now I want to kill her myself."

"No, I didn't kill her." She looked down at the floor and gulped. "What I did was worse.

"Mother had prepared a place for Chris. A secret tomb in the basement of the house we lived in. It was there, and ready. I covered her face; I couldn't look at her. She knew what I was doing. Jason helped me drag her into the tomb. We bricked the wall up. I threw her magic book in with her and used a spell to hide what I'd done. Then we left.

"I left her to die, Chris. I left our mother to die."

"That's nothing less than she had planned to do to Chris," said Ana defiantly. "I'm glad for what you did."

"So whatever we felt tonight, and whoever we suspect may be controlling Harrison, it can't be her, Chris. It can't. I left her in that place."

"And that's why you never let me go back there. You were afraid I'd feel her presence."

"Yes. After we finished, Jason helped me pack up my things, and I went to his house. We called you, and you met us there the next day. And that was that. Neither Jason nor I ever went back. The house was just abandoned. I never checked it again; Chris, did you?"

"Yes, I've kept my eye on it. I wanted to know if she returned or if there were any sign of magic about the place, but there's been nothing. The taxes were never paid, and it came up for auction a few years ago. No one bid on it. I think the evil she did there lingers, and that's what kept people away from it."

"We need to go check on it," said Dave.

"No! I don't want to go there."

"He's right, Shannon. We have to go. What's been happening here… what we both felt tonight. We both thought it felt like her."

"Similar, but different, too. You said so yourself, Chris. It wasn't exactly like Mother's vibes. It can't be her. There are a lot of evil things in the world, and I'm sure they all give off a similar aura. She's behind that wall in the basement in Chicago. At least her corpse is."

"You said you threw her book in with her?" questioned Dave.

"Yes, I didn't want anyone else getting their hands on it."

"She could have… it's a long shot, but you say she was powerful."

"What?"

"I hate to say it, but even bound as you say, she might have been able to access her book with her mind."

"No! Oh no."

"Well, anyway, we can't go tomorrow. It's summer solstice. we have to be available to stop anything the Artificial Witch might try. We have to stop these murders."

"Okay, but Shannon, the day after we're going to Chicago. You need to know exactly what happened to your mother. It's hanging like the Sword of Damocles over your head—yours and Chris's both. Whatever the outcome, you need to know."

"He's right. And you aren't going alone. Chris and I are coming with you," said Ana.

CHAPTER 39

It was 4 o'clock on a hot, Kentucky summer afternoon, the Summer Solstice, the longest day of the year. Heat waves rolled up from the black top as Winnie let herself out the back door of The Wolf's Den.

"See you tonight, Abby. Thanks for letting me off early to get ready," she called.

"Not a problem," Abby said. "I'll see you later."

"I wouldn't miss it." She shut the door of the shop, turned toward the parking lot, and jumped in surprise.

"Salvia! I didn't see you there," she said as the woman appeared, almost on top of her.

"Oh Winnie, I'm so glad I caught you. I wanted to invite you over for a drink and a talk. I know you've been having a hard time lately, and I just thought we might chat a little bit about empowerment and how some of my meditation practices might help you."

Winnie pulled her phone from her pocket and checked the time. Yes, she had plenty of time to talk with Salvia before she got ready for the evening's celebration. "Sure," she said. "Let me just text my friend that I'll be a little late. I was going to meet him."

"Oh, I'm sure it won't take that long, you don't need to text anyone."

But Winnie quickly shot a message to Tyler. *"With Salvia. If u don't c me later tell Dave."* She was sure the woman was just trying to be nice, but just in case, Tyler was her safety net.

~~~

It was over an hour later when Shannon and Dave pulled into the parking lot. They planned to stake out the stores and follow Harrison and Salvia wherever they went. Tony and Jake were in an unmarked vehicle at the front of the store. The chief had wanted to be sure they had both exits covered.

"Do you seen anything?" Tony's voice crackled over the car's radio.

"Not a thing. It's quiet as a tomb back here. Abby's car is still here, as well as Harrison's motorcycle and a couple of other cars—probably grocery store employees. "Do we know what Salvia drives?" asked Dave.

"According to Motor Vehicles she has a Jeep SUV. Older model, black."

"Yep, it's still here."

About 6 p.m. they watched as Abby came out of her shop, locked the door, and headed to her car. "Abby's coming out the door of her shop now," Dave said.

"Well that's one person we don't have to worry about. She told me she'd be heading straight to Cassandra's from here," said Jake.

Shannon quickly switched off the mic and turned to Dave, eyebrows raised. "Jake talked to Abby? He wasn't supposed to say anything to anyone. Since when are the two of them so close that he's confiding department business?"

"You got me. He never said anything. Well good for them if they are."

"I know but…"

"Are you upset that Jake said something to Abby, or that Abby hasn't said anything to you about Jake?" Dave asked. He laughed when she made a face at him, "Well, I'm getting it out of her tomorrow morning," she said as they settled back and continued to watch in silence.

The minutes ticked slowly by. Shannon ran her hand through her sweaty hair. A breeze wafted through the window; unfortunately, it brought the odor of the dumpster on the other side of the parking lot with it. A couple of teenagers headed in the back door of the grocery store then came out a few minutes later, a bag with chips sticking out of a plastic shopping bag in one of their hands.

No one came out of Baubles and Beads, and no one went in. It was almost 7 p.m. The heat was finally beginning to recede a bit. It wouldn't be dark for over an hour though.

"I'm sorry you're missing the Summer Solstice

ceremonies," Shannon said. "Will you be in trouble?"

"No, Jake and I explained the importance of being here tonight. Cassandra wants this over with as much as any of the rest of us. The longer it goes on, the more chances there are of our exposure to the non-para community."

"Do you think we've missed them?" Tony's voice came over the radio.

"I don't know how they could have left. We've been here since before closing time, and their cars are still here," answered Dave.

"I wish we had a search warrant. We could go inside."

"I could check if the door's open," said Shannon. "I can pretend I want to buy something and check the door that way."

"Sounds good. Come around to the front though," Tony told her.

Shannon walked around to the front of the store and tried the door. It was locked. She rattled the knob, peered in through the window, and finally called out, "Salvia? It's me, Shannon. Are you there?"

Finally she turned away, shrugged her shoulders at Jake and Tony in their car across the street, and walked back around the building.

"I'm starting to get a bad feeling about this," Dave said into his microphone when he saw Shannon returning. "At least I know Winnie is safely out of the way. Abby was going to let her go early tonight."

Shannon got back in the car and they sat silently as time seemed to drag slower and slower. It was after 9 p.m. and had finally grown dark when a car roared into the parking lot, startling Dave and Shannon, who had all of their attention focused on the back door of the store. Two car doors slammed shut, and Tyler and Chris got out.

"Winnie's missing," Tyler called as he ran toward them.

Dave jumped out of his vehicle. "What the hell do you mean, Winnie's missing?" he shouted.

"I mean Winnie's missing! She was supposed to meet me at 8 o'clock, and she never came. She sent me a text late this afternoon."

Tyler held out his phone. Dave snatched it from his hand. *"With Salvia. If u don't c me later tell Dave,"* he read aloud for Shannon to hear. "Damn it, damn it, damn it! I told that girl to stay away from all this." Dave ran his hand through his hair.

Shannon switched on the car's mic. "Tony, Jake, get back here. We have a problem."

A minute later their car rounded the corner and stopped by the other police vehicle. "What's going on?" Jake asked as they got out of the car.

"We missed them, damn it. And they've got Winnie!" Dave slammed his fist on the hood of his vehicle.

"How?" asked Jake.

"They must have been gone before we even got here. They left the lights on so we'd think they were still there."

"Why didn't you go inside and check?" asked Tyler.

Dave glared at him. "The door was locked. There's a thing called a search warrant, Kid. We had no legal reason to get a warrant."

"But…"

Chris put his hand on Tyler's arm, giving him a warning look. "Okay, now that we know they have Winnie, what's the plan?"

"We still can't get a warrant," said Jake as Dave slammed the car hood one more time. "But we now have a legitimate reason to enter the store. It's well after closing time, and all the lights are on. Maybe someone has broken in."

"Do you think they have her in there?" Tyler asked.

The four cops got their vests out of the car trunks and were putting them on as Dave answered. "I've got no idea, but I'm going to find out." As he walked toward the back door, Tyler started to follow. Dave turned around and glared at him. "Stay!" he said.

Chris put a restraining hand on Tyler's arm, and Shannon sent him a sympathetic look.

"Dave and Shannon, you wait here until we get back around to the front of the store. We'll go in at the same time," Tony told them. He and Jake took off at a run. A minute later

Shannon's mic crackled. "We're in position."

Dave pulled his gun and shouted, "Police, open up!" He tried the door, and when he found it locked, motioned with his hands and whispered an incantation. Shannon tried the door as soon as he finished and this time and it opened silently.

They let Tony and Jake in the front door and the four cops searched the store quickly. It was obvious that no one was there, but the back room where Salvia held her meetings looked as if there had been a struggle. Chairs were turned over; the fabric that had covered the shelves during the empowerment meetings was heaped on the floor. Shannon felt sick looking at the mess. Where was Winnie? Had she been hurt? They headed out the back door where Chris and Tyler waited for them.

"She's not there," said Dave.

Tyler slumped against the car. "What do we do now?" he asked.

CHAPTER 40

"You don't do anything, Kid," said Tony. "You and Chris need to stay right here."

"I don't think so. We know now that Harrison has some power, and he may be working with someone who has more," said Chris. "I've got jurisdiction if it involves something paranormal. And Tyler's a werewolf. He could be useful."

"You, maybe," Tony replied. "But he's a kid. He's got no business…"

"They've got Winnie. It is my business. And if I hadn't waited so long…"

"They would still have had her," Shannon told him, putting a hand on his shoulder. "They had her minutes after she texted you. I'm just glad she had a chance to send it, and that you took it seriously."

"But…"

"Whatever! Let's not stand here arguing about this!" Dave said. "They're probably at the Indian Mounds; that's where the other murders have been. Let's get there as fast as we can." He headed to the car, jumping in the driver's seat although it was usually Shannon who drove when they were on patrol.

"Chris, I don't have time to stop you from following after us, and I don't have time to worry about whether or not you bring Tyler along. Just stay out of our way unless something happens that we need to call on you for back up."

"Fine. Let's go. Shannon, take care of yourself."

The three cars headed toward the river, going as fast as possible in two unmarked cars without sirens. "We'll stop and coordinate once we get about two miles from the park entrance," Tony said over the microphone.

"Roger," replied Shannon. They rode on in a tense silence, Dave's knuckles white as he gripped the wheel. Shannon didn't know how to comfort him. He was terrified for his cousin, and so was she.

It took less than twenty minutes to get within two miles of the entrance to the park. They pulled over to the side of the road. Chris pulled in after them. Shannon noticed he had Tyler stay in the car. Out of sight, out of mind, she thought. She knew Tyler wasn't going to stay behind, and if the others forgot about him, Chris wouldn't have to try and make him.

"Look," said Tony, "the last time we found a body it wasn't too far past the entrance. The gate's going to be shut..."

"I'll handle that," Dave interrupted.

"Fine, just make sure it's quiet. We'll park just inside the gate, then make our way on foot. Chris, I want you and Tyler to stay well behind us. I'd tell you to stay in your car, but I know that's not going to happen."

Chris nodded and headed back to his vehicle as the others got back in theirs. They drove slowly now, and when they approached the gate, Dave stopped the car, chanted for a moment under his breath, and the gate swung noiselessly open.

"You've got to teach me that one, too," Shannon said, admiration in her voice. Dave just nodded, pulled through, and stopped the car, the other vehicles behind him.

As they got out, they could hear a voice chanting in the distance. Behind them, Jake called for backup. It was too far away to tell if it were a man or a woman. As they crept closer, Shannon could make out the figure of Harrison standing over a makeshift altar of wood. Winnie lay, naked, tied to it; there was blood on her torso and Shannon could see a gash on her head. The girl didn't move. Just How badly was she hurt? Shannon prayed they weren't too late. She looked around for Salvia and saw the woman tied to a tree not far away.

Suddenly Shannon sensed another presence. Someone else was here, someone hidden from her. Was it the same presence she and Chris had felt at the restaurant the night before? Who... or what... was it?

Salvia noticed them as they crept slowly forward, and her eyes grew wide. Shannon shook her head and put her finger to her lips. Salvia nodded.

Shannon gestured that she would untie Salvia while the three other officers took on Harrison.

She turned and saw Chris and Tyler melting into the shadows as they quietly got into position also. So much for the two of them staying out of the way. "Stay safe," she whispered, even knowing she was too far away for her brother to hear her.

She had no idea what they were all getting into. The only thing she knew was that Harrison and at least one more entity were here. Four to two—or six if you counted Chris and Tyler. It should be more than enough, but who knew what type of power they were up against?

Shannon circled around Salvia and came up behind her. "Don't make a sound; I'm going to set you free," she whispered as she drew out a knife and cut the ropes that bound the woman. She pulled her farther into the trees so they could whisper without anyone hearing. "Is there anyone here besides Harrison?"

"Yes... no... I don't know. I haven't seen anyone, but Harrison keeps talking to someone. I think he's lost his mind, Shannon."

Noise broke out behind them, and Shannon heard Jake's voice. "This is the police. Move back from the girl."

"I've got to go help them, Salvia. Can you quietly head to the parking lot? Don't run. It's too dark, and you'll just trip over something."

Salvia nodded. "Shannon, I didn't know. You've got to believe me; I really didn't know," she said and turned to walk away.

Shannon moved toward the clearing. She couldn't see Chris or Tyler but knew they must be somewhere nearby. She could hear the commotion before her but sensed another presence even closer. She turned quickly. Nothing.

It must be her imagination. It had to be. She still wasn't that good at sensing power, especially if it were cloaked.

She continued on.

Just as she got within sight of the clearing, all hell broke loose. She watched Dave as he headed for Winnie to free her. Shannon drew a sigh of relief. Winnie was crying; she was still alive.

Tony called, "You're under arrest."

"No, you can't have her. She's mine. My sacrifice," cried Harrison. "She was promised to me. Every time I sacrifice a victim I gain power. She promised me. She's promised me."

Even as he cried out, he turned toward Dave, and Shannon could see the gun in his hand. Tony and Jake were too far away. Shannon struck out instinctively. She had to save Dave.

"Incantare Thanatos," she shouted a moment after Harrison's gun went off. Harrison fell to the ground, unable to move, but Dave stumbled backward and fell, too.

For the next few moments everything was a jumbled mess. Chris was trying to hold Tyler back, but he broke free and ran toward Winnie. Sharp claws sprouted from his hand, and he used them to cut through her bonds, grabbing her up in his arms. Shannon reached Dave just as quickly. He lay on the ground clutching his shoulder.

"Don't move. Don't move. You're bleeding."

"Damn bullet missed my vest. Hit me in the arm," he said.

"Shannon pushed his hand away and pressed on his wound to stem the blood. You're bleeding, Dave. Oh goddess, what if I can't stop it?"

"Shannon, stop, I'm alright. It's not that bad." Dave struggled to sit up even as she pushed him back down.

"Call for an ambulance, Shannon." Tony came over to them and bent down to look at the wound. "It doesn't look too bad, Dave."

"I know," he replied. "Shannon, you hear that? It's not bad. I'm not Jason, Shannon. I'm not going to bleed out on you. I'm staying right here with you."

She took a breath and nodded. "You'd better mean that," she said, then took out her phone and called for an ambulance.

At that moment Winnie, with Tyler's arm around her,

made it to David's side. Tyler had taken off his shirt and covered her with it, but Shannon could still see the bloody wounds on her torso.

"Oh goddess, are you hurt bad?" Winnie asked, leaning down to hug Dave.

"I should be asking you that," he said.

"I'm fine, I'm fine." Tears fell down her cheeks. "Thank you all for coming to save me. He's crazy. Harrison's crazy. He was going to sacrifice me."

CHAPTER 41

It was almost dawn before everyone was able to convene again in Winnie's hospital room. Ambulances had taken Dave and her to the hospital shortly after they arrived at the scene. But it had taken a lot longer for the forensics staff to clear the area, for Salvia and Harrison to be booked, and for everyone else involved to make their statements.

Dave was treated and released for the bullet graze in his shoulder. Winnie was being kept for at least one day. She had several knife wounds, and while none seemed too deep, she'd been in shock by the time they got to the hospital. The doctors said she wouldn't have any scars. At least no physical ones.

"Salvia is claiming she knows nothing about the three murders or the kidnapping and attack on Winnie," Tony told them when he arrived to see how Winnie was doing. "She remembers talking to Winnie in the parking lot, but says she remembers nothing else until she woke up and saw Shannon walking toward her in the woods. We suspect her memory was blocked using spells, but since she's going to be tried in a non-para court, it won't help her. She'll be charged as an accessory. Maybe she can plead insanity and serve her time in a mental institution."

"Couldn't someone unblock her memory?" asked Winnie.

"It's tricky, Honey," said Dave. "Since she is a non-para, unblocking her memory might leave her with more mental scars than she has already."

"We know everything Harrison did was pretty gruesome, and we suspect he may have been using her in more ways than just having her help or even just witness the murders," explained Jake. "The story he told Dave about the money for the store coming from him turns out to be false. It was her money all along, and he was stealing it."

"Her intentions were good," said Shannon.

"I'll see what can be done to help her, maybe get her a lighter sentence," said her brother. "That's part of my job as a Hunter; to mitigate any harm done to non-paras."

"Harrison is also claiming it wasn't his fault. Says he was possessed by some unknown 'supernatural' being," added Tony. "It may be true, but he'll go to trial. It will be as a non-para as well, and I think in his case he'll probably get sentenced to an insane asylum. I think that's where he belongs—if he didn't before whatever went on here happened, he certainly does now. We'll try to get him sentenced to somewhere run by paranormals, so he can be treated for possession. Who knows? It might help him."

"But who—or what—possessed him?" asked Winnie. Shannon and her brother exchanged glances. They were afraid they knew.

A nurse entered the room and shooed everyone out, saying it was time for Winnie to rest. Shannon and Dave headed back to her home as the sun was rising on another bright summer day.

"I can't believe it's all over," said David.

"I hope it really is. But we won't know until we go to Chicago."

"Whatever we find, remember, I'll be there for you," David said as they entered her house through the back door. He turned her to face him, kissing her tenderly. "Are you ready for bed?" he asked.

"Bed, or sleep?"

"Bed," he replied.

"Lead the way."

Upstairs, Shannon stood at the edge of the bed, gazing at Dave as the sunlight streamed in the window, affirming that she was no longer living in the dark.

He was waiting, patient, but his eyes held the same fiery intensity that had sparked their connection from the start. She moved toward him, the feeling of power in her veins, her magic flowing like a river ready to burst its banks. The battle was over, the mystery unraveled, but the bond between them had deepened in ways she couldn't have predicted.

Dave reached out, pulling her close, his hands warm against her skin. His lips brushed her temple, the touch gentle yet possessive.

Shannon's breath hitched as he trailed his lips down her neck, the soft pressure igniting a spark that spread through her body, all the way to her core. Her hand curled into the back of his shirt, pulling him closer, her hips pressing into his.

The world around them seemed to melt away. There was just the two of them, raw and real. He lifted her effortlessly, and she straddled his lap, her legs wrapping around his waist as their lips met in a kiss that was both desperate and tender. The bond between them pulsed with energy, their power intertwining like threads of light, igniting something deeper.

She could feel the strength of his desire; her hands moved over his back, tracing the lines of his tattoos—symbols of strength and survival.

"Shannon, no more secrets. No more walls. I love you. I want you."

Her heart raced as she looked into his eyes, seeing not just the desire but the promise of forever. She could feel the bond between them, magical and undeniable, and she knew without a doubt, that this was where she was meant to be. They would face the future together. No matter what they learned tomorrow.

EPILOGUE

They didn't make it to Chicago for almost a week. It took a few days for all of the paperwork and interviews regarding the Artificial Witch case to be wrapped up. Dave and Shannon would end up testifying at the trials, but at least for now they could spend a few days relaxing.

Dave still had another few days of sick leave after his injury, Ana had recently quit her job at the University. She would be teaching second grade at a local elementary school in the fall and wanted some time off to spend with Chris and Sophie before the new job started.

Dave and Ana were concerned for Shannon and Chris, but they didn't really understand the depth of the fear the brother and sister had as they headed to their old home.

"I'm sure it will be fine," Ana kept saying, as they travelled the half-day's drive up U.S. 41 to Illinois. Chris was driving and Ana was sitting next to him. In the back seat Shannon rolled her eyes. Learning Dave's white magic had brought back memories of many of the not-so-white spells her mother had taught her as a child. If Ana said it would be fine one more time, Shannon was considering stealing her voice—just for a little while.

She didn't really mean it. Ana was so good for her brother, and she was just trying to be supportive. Dave obviously sensed what she was thinking. He squeezed her hand, and whispered, "No, no, no. You don't use black magic anymore." He was laughing at her. She didn't even have to look at him to know; his humor made this whole trip bearable.

In Chicago, they braved the usual traffic jams and made their way to their old neighborhood. Never the best, it hadn't improved with age. Their old home was not the only abandoned house on the street, and even the ones that were occupied looked shabby.

The four of them got out of the car, Dave and Ana

standing back so Chris and Shannon could go at their own pace. The concrete steps led to a wooden porch with holes they had to navigate. They didn't have to worry about breaking the lock—there was none.

They opened the door and entered. Obviously, squatters, both human and animal, had used the place. There was trash and filth everywhere.

"I guess you have to lead the way," Chris said apologetically. "You're the only one who knows the spell to show us where…" he stopped and gulped, unable to go on.

Shannon nodded. She understood Chris's reluctance. She slowly led them down the basement steps, but as soon as she got to the bottom, she knew there was no need for magical assistance. The wall behind which she had placed her mother was broken open. The concrete she and Jason had used to close the hole lay in shattered blocks strewn across the floor. She and Chris stopped, frozen. Dave moved forward, brushing her shoulder with his hand as he passed, and peered inside the hole.

"There's nothing there," he said. "It's empty. There's no body. No book of spells. Nothing."

ACKNOWLEDGMENTS

Dear Reader,

I hope you are enjoying my Unleashed series—complete with sexy werewolves, witches and vampires, oh my! I hope you have as much fun reading it as I have had writing it.

I knew Shannon needed her own happily ever after as soon as I wrote her first line of dialogue in *The Hunter's Moon*. It took more time for Dave, her perfect match, to come to life.

If you like Rivelou and all of its inhabitants, both paranormal and non-para, you'll be happy to know I have more books in the works. Dan, Ana's big brother, and Nathan Lazard, our vampire, and of course Ana's happy-go-lucky friend Monica, will all be finding their mates soon. I wonder what Monica's going to say when she finds out werewolves are real—and that her best friend is one.

And what about Channing and Dolan? Channing's playing with fire, don't you think? I'll let you in on a little secret. I'd planned to kill Winnie in this book but my editor forced me to reconsider. She loved Winnie too much, so she'll be getting her own happy-ever-after.

Now for the thank you's. First, I want to thank you, my readers, for choosing to purchase my books and read and review them. An independent author's lifeblood is good reviews, so I hope you will go to https://amzn.to/4jqKsCh and give me a review.

I also need to thank my excellent editor, Cheryl Garayta for not only reading and critiquing my work, but for being willing to listen to my new ideas and tell me when they are either great or terrible. And again, to Sherri A. Lynn, Janice Detrie, and Wendy Wyatt for all their hard work as my beta readers. To Noelle Stary and Nicole Loughan for listening and cheering me on. And to Eric Labacz who always comes up with better artwork than I can ever imagine. His covers are wonderful.

I couldn't do it without all of you.

ABOUT THE AUTHOR

Lee K. Rogers has been reading fantasy since she discovered the Brothers Grimm, and her love of the genre has only grown from there. From classics such as the Narnia series and *The Lord of the Rings* (before the movies came out of course!) to Charlaine Harris' series, Pamela Clare, and of course Rebecca Yarros—she reads it all. When she discovered urban fantasy romance she found her passion. She particularly loves adding a little spicy sex to her fantasy adventures.

In her other life, Lee's name is Karen Hodges Miller and she writes books designed to help other self-published authors achieve success. She once lived in the Kentucky/Indiana border town on which she has modeled Rivelou. You'll get some clues as to which town it is when reading the books. While she never met a werewolf there, she was convinced there was an entrance to the land of Fae just down the street from her house.

The Hunter's Moon is the first in her paranormal romance series, Unleashed. *The Artificial Witch* is book two, and book three, *The Wolf Revealed, will be out in July, 2025.*

She is still working on her various social media connections. You can connect with her on Facebook at https://www.facebook.com/profile.php?id=61570087745394 and on Blue Sky https://bsky.app/profile/leekrogers.bsky.social. Here website is www.LeeKRogers.com

Want to read more about the paranormals of Rivelou? Dan's story is next. Pre-order The Wolf Revealed, available on July 22, 2025.
https://www.amazon.com/Wolf-Revealed-Unleashed-Paranormal-Fantasy-ebook/dp/B0DVLTSNCY

www.ingramcontent.com/pod-product-compliance
Lightning Source LLC
Chambersburg PA
CBHW07082718O626
46818CB00001B/421